"As much as I don't want to, I think we'd better say good-night."

Her warmth slipped away with her, leaving his arms empty and cold.

"I do believe you're right, ma'am. Now's as good a time as any." The minute their hands touched, he wanted to forget all good intentions and hold her to him once more. From the longing in her expression, she felt the same. Sarah had given him all sorts of reasons to change the life he'd grown to love. His aloneness had become just that—alone. And he didn't like it anymore. Yet her reputation in town would be ruined if he didn't leave, and right this second. "Yes, well, good night, then."

One thing was for certain and for sure. He had to figure out a way for her to keep the farm and for him to let God know he planned to honor his promise—but with a wife at his side.

Books by Linda S. Glaz

Love Inspired Heartsong Presents

With Eyes of Love
Always, Abby
The Substitute Bride
The Preacher's New Family

LINDA S. GLAZ

Linda, married with three grown children and three grandchildren, is a complete triple-A personality. How else would she find time to write as well as be an agent for Hartline Literary Agency? She loves any and everything about the written word, and loves families passing stories along through the generations. If she isn't writing or putting together a contract, you'll find her taking a relaxing bath with her eReader in hand.

LINDA S. GLAZ

The Preacher's New Family

HEARTSONG
PRESENTS

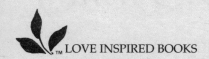 LOVE INSPIRED BOOKS

Recycling programs for this product may not exist in your area.

ISBN-13: 978-0-373-48700-4

THE PREACHER'S NEW FAMILY

Copyright © 2014 by Linda S. Glaz

www.Harlequin.com

Printed in U.S.A.

He heals the brokenhearted and binds up their wounds.
—*Psalms* 147:3

To everyone who has ever suffered a broken heart, who, with help from the Lord, has learned to start over.

Chapter 1

Dakota Territory, 1881

The prairie was a cold mistress. But TJ loved her none-theless, loved the freedom to come and go, no questions asked. It did his heart good, like a tonic. Never again would he be jammed twelve to a room as he had been in the slums of New York City.

Terrance Jonathan O'Brien, TJ to his friends—few as they were—poured the last drops of coffee into his tin cup. As he wrapped his hands around the warmth and sipped the strong, hot goodness, his gaze surveyed the open expanse of land. He took another sip, remembering the tough times after his folks had passed on.

Five years ago, when he had turned twenty-one and Uncle Michael had given him the $200 from his parents and a handful of keepsakes, TJ had left New York, and it had been the best day of his life—up to now. Sitting here, gazing over the prairie, he soaked in the kind of freedom only open space could provide.

TJ set down his cup and stretched the kinks out of his legs. It had been a long day's ride. He breathed deeply of the dusty prairie. Clear, uncluttered land. No people, no noises except that of the earth and its diminutive creatures. Crickets shouted a round of chirps, and he smiled at the interruption the noisy little critters caused in his thoughts. The sound of crickets he could tolerate; the noises of humanity, not quite as much. But in his calling as a preacher, he'd have to listen plenty.

Peaceful and free. How he loved the opportunity to pick up and go whenever he chose. He could stop for a day or two and appreciate a cold spring, a tree in the middle of nowhere, a rabbit that would soon roast crackling over an open fire then fill his belly. Never again would he listen to neighbors screaming at each other and pounding on common walls—unhappy families fighting over a scrap of space to sleep or a loaf of bread to eat.

For two years now, he'd been preaching God's Word to anyone who itched to pull up a chair and listen. An empty schoolhouse in one town, a saloon in another. Maybe a neighbor's front porch with blankets as pews. Didn't matter so long as TJ could breeze into town, preach and hightail it out of there before some well-meaning mother presented her unmarried daughter for the preacher's appreciation. Each town seemed to have an unlimited number of unmarried females looking for a sorry single fella without the sense to say no. But not this fella. The last thing he wanted was to be tied down to some anxious girl with family on her mind. No, sirree...not TJ.

Tomorrow he'd arrive in Gullywash, the town he'd recently been invited to make part of his circuit. He prayed for plenty of welcoming folks willing to listen, but not enough so that he'd feel penned in. This life presented a delicate balance between his desire for seclusion and the needs of the folks. After all, his entire reason for living was to bring the love of God to the lost, the same way it had been brought to him.

He lifted the coffeepot from the fire and sat up straight. Snaking his hand into his saddlebag, he drew out the Bible his uncle had given him when TJ had learned to read. His thumbs caressed the cover. Soft, worn leather slid beneath his touch. The words, etched on his heart, fulfilled every desire of his life. He was comfortable in the solitude of his simple life.

"Mama, Mama, Mama! A man's a-comin'. A big man. On a horse. Near our well. Mama, Mama. C'mere, quick! He looks awful mean."

Sarah Anne Rycroft jumped from her rocker, sending her son's half-patched pants—needle still stuck in the leg—sliding to the floor. She dashed for the fireplace mantel and, stretching on the toes of her boots, hefted her late husband's Winchester from the rack. Her fingers trembled as she readied herself to fire if necessary. "Get away from the window and get in your room, Zach." Breath caught in her throat. "Now!"

As her son scampered away, Sarah dashed to the front, opened the door a crack and peered around the edge of the thick maple wood. A tall man with a rough day-old beard, dressed in a long black duster, black hat, black gloves and black boots, rode high in the saddle on a bay horse that must have been eighteen hands, at least. She hadn't ever seen a bigger bay, and such an imposing, intimidating figure on its back. Zach was right—the man looked…well, menacing. "Who's there?" she called.

The man pulled a glove off and waved a hand. "May I have a dipper of water, miss?"

"Mrs. Mrs. Rycroft. My husband's gone to town, but he should be back any second. If you're wanting a drink, go ahead, and then move on along." She made sure to let the barrel of the rifle stick out the door far enough so there would be no funny business or further questions.

"Yes, ma'am. If I'm not putting you out too much, I'd like to fill my canteen and water my horse, and I'd thank you kindly for the hospitality. It's a scorcher today and I'm afraid my horse is mighty thirsty."

Sarah stepped onto the porch, the gray weathered boards creaking slightly, the rifle heavy in her grip as she watched the man lead the bay closer to the well. Then she felt a spark of guilt over her lack of compassion for the stranger passing through her property. Nathaniel would be upset at her behavior. If he could see her standing there, ready to shoot the man through the heart, he'd have words with her.

"You new to these parts?" she asked.

"Yes'm. Riding in to see the sheriff. He's a friend of mine."

Sheriff Redford. He and his wife, Molly, were friends of hers, too. "You had breakfast today?"

"A couple of corn dodgers and leftover roasted rabbit when I rose."

The sun burned straight overhead, shooting blinding rays, reminders that the man had likely gotten up six hours ago. Nathaniel had always been able to eat as much as she could cook, and this fellow probably had a powerful hunger by now. "What's your name? What are you doing in these parts?"

"TJ, ma'am. I'm the new circuit rider. I'll be in town over Sunday to preach. Didn't mean to frighten your boy."

Since when did Gullywash have a preacher?

"This'll be my first time here. Sheriff Redford invited me when he picked up a prisoner last month and heard me in the pulpit. I guess I do all right according to some folks."

Nice-looking man for a preacher, but too young to be able to understand what was in his Bible…which was nothing. Nothing that made any sense to her. Not anymore. And besides, looks had little to do with it. So what?

However, the hat, gloves, black jacket—why, the sun must be baking him alive. She should at least be polite. After settling the rifle against the side of the door, she put a hand to her forehead and shaded her eyes. She attempted a smile but realized it must look painted on her face; she hadn't smiled much lately. "You look mighty green to be a preacher. Can't be much older than I am. How do you expect to teach folks?"

"I can assure you, I'm old enough to preach and then some." He slipped out of the saddle and Sarah reached for the rifle again.

She bit the side of her lip, trying to decide whether or not to give the man some bread and honey, when she heard a scream. "Mah-ma!"

Sarah spun around and she dropped the rifle to the

porch with a loud crash. The scream had come from the back of the house. She dashed down the porch two steps at a time and ran around the side of the house, where she froze. Her spindly four-year-old clung to the edge of the roof, fingers clawing to keep from falling. He screamed her name. "Mama, catch me. I can't hold on no more!"

"Zach!" Her feet froze to the ground. *Not again. God, please, not again. I can't lose my baby, too.*

With the charge of a bull, the preacher pushed past her. He stopped below Zach and held up both arms. "Drop down, boy. C'mon. I'll catch you."

"Mama? Mama! I'm falling!"

"Let go. I've got you." The preacher reached both arms up, his fingers nearly touching Zach's feet. The span of his limbs was near as wide as a sturdy tree's.

Sarah's heart thundered in her ears as her precious boy dropped into the man's grasp. She rushed to their side, her arms half around Zach and half around the stranger. She buried her face in Zach's teary face. "Oh, Zach, whatever were you doing up on the roof? You know better. Shame on you for scaring me. Are you sure you're all right?"

His tears dampened his shirt and he licked the moisture from his upper lip. "I climbeded up the tree and out on the roof. I was tryin' to p'tect you, Mama. Like Daddy. I had a rock I coulda throwed at that man if he hurt you." He dropped a threatening frown at the preacher and hugged Sarah tighter. "S-or-ry. I dinnunt mean to scare you." He looked at the big man with as much courage as fear—her four-year-old boy doing his best to take his father's place.

At first the preacher shot the boy a look mean as a

bear's, but all the time, he held tight. "Boy, you should obey your mama. You've scared her half to death." Then he smiled, a gentle smile that said all was forgiven and gave his forceful face a kind expression. "You all right, young fella?"

"Uh-huh. I'm sorry, Mama."

Sarah, lip quivering as much as Zach's, turned to the stranger. "Thank you, Mr…?"

The man pressed Zach into her arms and held out a hand. "O'Brien, ma'am. TJ O'Brien at your service. I have to say, you must be proud. One mighty brave fellow you have here."

"You certainly were at our service." She snuggled Zach closer until he arched his back and turned into the little man who had tried his best to take her husband's place as her protector.

"Mama, put me down. I'm not a baby."

He was definitely not a baby. In fact, he was growing up much too fast for her. Turning from blond to light brown, his curls had begun to look more and more like Nathaniel's hair, thick and silky and loaded with the smell of grass and sunshine. Oh, how she missed the love of that sweet man. From the day she had turned sixteen, he had been the one and only man in her life. Pa's hardest worker. Fresh hay and manure clung to his clothes most of the time. Sweat and sweetness. And he'd kissed her on her birthday. Yes, she saw Nathaniel in Zach's brown eyes every day.

A tear slipped down her cheek, and she swiped at it before she could embarrass herself further. Too late for that now—Zach and TJ had both seen.

The man's blue-gray eyes blinked in his handsome

face, which was filled with compassion. "Are you all right, ma'am?"

"I am, Mr. O'Brien. Won't you come in and have a bowl of soup and a piece of warm bread with honey? I do believe we can spare that much to show our appreciation." She headed back toward the porch and motioned for him to follow.

His face drew into a frown, but not until after he'd licked his lips at her mention of soup. "What about your husband, ma'am? Won't he be hungry when he gets home? I'd hate to finish his dinner for him."

Her footsteps drew to a halt. Her husband. Maybe... maybe he could be trusted. He was a preacher, after all.

"Mr. O'Brien. I apologize for my falsehood. Forgive me. I have to be careful out here alone. My husband passed on two years ago. You see here a sad excuse for a farmer and her son. I can shoot, at least, enough so we survive. And Zach—Zach takes care of the small animals on the farm."

"Animals?" He glanced around until she saw him notice the barn.

"Yes, two dozen chickens and five piglets for my son to see to, while I take care of the larger ones. Three cows, two calves and three horses. Two of the horses as fine a set as you'll see."

"Nice little spread."

"We get by. No luxuries to speak of, but we have plenty of food and lots of fresh milk for Zach." They did get by until the banker told her Nathaniel hadn't paid up on all the land. She either forked over the rest of the money by the end of September or she lost the farm.

Well, no need for the preacher to know about all their sorrows. That was tomorrow's problem, not today's.

"I'd be mighty grateful for a home-cooked meal, ma'am. If you're sure—"

"Please, Mr. O'Brien. Call me Sarah or Sarah Anne. The *ma'am* makes me feel older than my years." Older than her years. At Nathaniel's death she'd felt much more than twenty-three. And now, two long, hard years later, she felt like an old woman, and probably looked like one, too. She couldn't help reaching up to tuck loose strands of hair behind her ear. In spite of feeling as if she were betraying Nathaniel, she couldn't help but notice the fine features of the preacher man. Even after a long, dusty ride, he looked good.

"Then you'll have to call me TJ. All my friends do." He held out a warm, callused hand. Her skin tingled when she touched him. "And we'll be able to call ourselves friends once we break bread and I help with the chores to pay you back."

"Oh, no. I couldn't let you do that. You saved Zachary. I'm the one obliged."

"Yes, ma'am. The only way I'd feel right to impose. I pay my own way."

Sarah nodded and picked up the fallen rifle on the way into her house. As they entered, TJ took it from her and placed it back over the mantel. She shivered as their hands touched.

"Again, please forgive my unkind welcome. And it's thoughtful of you to offer your help." She indicated their seats, making sure she kept a nice comfortable distance from him. It would feel good to let someone else do her chores for a day. Maybe she'd even feed him supper…if he did a good day's work.

Mr. O'Brien took their hands and bowed his head. She pulled against his grasp, but he held tight. That's right; a preacher would want to pray. Well, she could close her eyes and pretend the God he was praying to hadn't taken away her wonderful husband. And she could ask forgiveness for allowing the preacher's hand to feel warm and comforting around hers for the third time in the past few minutes.

The lady's hand squeezed his fingers in a way that sent shocks of surprise straight through him. TJ peeked from under his brow. Obviously uncomfortable with prayers, she squirmed in her seat. And the little fellow gazed around the room as if he'd never heard a prayer spoken before.

These were hurting folks. But he had to remember that lots of folks were hurting hereabouts; these two had no more right to his time than anyone else. No man to take care of them. The lady a mere bit of a thing. He groaned at the direction his mind veered. He had to help with chores and move along. This was exactly why he chose to travel around. No staying in one place long enough to get attached to folks.

This weekend he'd be preaching in Gullywash and staying in the sheriff's guest room. Once a month, he'd make his modest circuit, preach, collect enough to keep him in coffee and then make the round again. Absolutely no one to tie him to any one place.

The delicious smells of beef soup, warm bread and hot coffee mingling together invaded his thoughts and prayers until he lost the battle. "Amen."

The soft voice mimicked his. "Amen."

"A-man, too," Zach added. "What's that mean, Mama? Why you guys talkin' about a man?"

Sarah's face zinged. "Zach. That's impolite to question our guest." She turned to TJ, red-faced. "I'm sorry. Since Nathaniel passed, I'm afraid I've allowed him more freedom to express himself to adults."

"Don't pay it any mind, ma'am. I'll explain to him after we eat. Uh, Sarah. If you don't mind."

She looked him in the eye and said, "I don't mind. It's most kind of you."

He blew out a huge unexpected sigh and picked up his spoon. "Smells mighty fine, ma'am."

She gazed anywhere but at him as she sliced the bread. Probably just as ill at ease with his presence as he was with hers. Only she looked very fine for being uneasy. Very fine indeed.

The boy giggled and clapped his hands. "Oh, boy. You gonna tell me about a man?"

"Zach." She patted the boy's hand.

TJ grinned at the happy little face. He leaned toward Sarah. "Be happy to oblige, Sarah. Youngsters out on the prairie don't often get to see a preacher. They're curious, is all." Her name slid off his lips like honey. He fought against the growl in his chest. He'd eat, talk to the boy, chop a load of wood to pay for the meal and make for town. The spacious room, full of homey knickknacks, had become stuffy. He had the sense it was closing in on him. He tugged at his collar as a piece of the sweet, warm bread stuck in his throat. He grabbed his coffee and choked it down.

The inviting home, the kindness of this woman, the freckle-faced boy. All three suddenly added to his discomfort. He didn't want these feelings. Didn't want attachments.

With a slight clearing of his throat, he took another swig.

"You okay, mis-ter?" Zach asked. "You look kinda funny."

Nowhere near as funny as he felt.

Chapter 2

Sheriff Redford clapped TJ on the back, his smile broad and genuine. "Have a seat, Preacher."

TJ pulled the heavy wooden chair away from the sheriff's desk. "I haven't thanked you properly for inviting me, Sheriff. When Tuscala got a live-in preacher, I was short one town each month. I appreciate you asking me to come here. Folks have seemed friendly enough these past two days."

"They are that and then some. We got happy and sad, cranky and glad, like any other town, I expect, but I like to think the people of Gullywash are special. Won't be long we'll need our own live-in preacher, as you call it." He grabbed the coffee off the stove. "Have another cup?"

TJ nodded. "Well, the sad ones are what I come around for. Reach 'em for Jesus before their lives are all muddled up."

The sheriff leaned in as close as he could get with his big belly keeping the distance. "Well, now. I expect you'll be reachin' 'em, but take it easy. Don't rain down all that fire and brimstone. Last man who preached here scared one woman near to death. He had his say only two times and then he moved on. I sort of figured you as a calmer man. One who shows folks the love of God instead of scarin' the all-fired sin outta them."

TJ couldn't stop the smile. "Then we're in agreement. I don't do well on fire and brimstone, either. Not my way. I heard plenty of that as a kid and fortunately, it didn't frighten me near to death *or* away from the good Lord. I figure a man learns as well when he sees how believing folks live their lives as he learns from what they say. I aim to live mine to show God's love." He tightened his fingers around the cup, remembering the folks who'd been turned away from the church in New York City because they had been dressed in dirty old clothes and not much else. The man had preached a good message, but only if you were his kind of person. And that meant money. "This is real good coffee. Mine is somewhat lacking. Always full of grounds."

Redford laughed. "Mine was, too, till my wife taught me how to brew a good cup. Drink up. Enjoy, Preacher. Maybe I'll teach you some tricks of the trade to take with you before you leave on Tuesday." He chuckled. "That is, if you preach a good sermon. Don't go scarin' the old folks."

"I'll do my best, and I'd be mighty obliged to learn your tricks."

TJ heard footsteps on the boardwalk out front and turned. The sheriff's gaze followed his. "That there's Sarah Anne Rycroft. Too young to be a widow lady.

She's one of the sad ones I was talkin' about. Raisin' a small boy all by herself."

"What happened to her husband?" His stomach did flips again, and he quickly sipped more of the strong coffee to quench the discomfort.

"He was dropped from a runaway horse. Ran into a large branch. Nearly took his head clean off. Killed him right out."

"That's horrible." She looked way too young to be a widow. And way too pretty for TJ's peace of mind.

"You never saw a woman carry on so. Like to break a person's heart. My wife took care of her for a couple weeks. The boy needed looking after and Mrs. Rycroft wasn't in any condition to see to his needs. Molly stayed up nights while both of them cried and carried on." He shook his head. "Heartbreaking's the only way to describe it."

"I met her at her farm. Day before yesterday. She's a kind lady, if not a tad cautious."

Redford's brow furrowed. "You met her, then? Yes, I heard tell she's a mite skittish out there alone. How'd she do, you bein' a stranger and all?"

"She was nice enough to let me water my horse. Gave me some soup and bread to go along with my dipper of water. Good soul."

The sheriff slapped a palm against his leg. "Well, I'll be. She nearly shot Caleb Mueller four months ago when he cut across her property. You must've made quite an impression. But you're right. She's a good soul even though she's been through a lot for such a young thing." He walked back to his chair. "So you all set to preach tomorrow?"

TJ clapped his hands together and grinned. "The widow's mite from Mark chapter 12."

"Ahh, and what inspired that message? Not the beautiful Mrs. Rycroft." Redford's eyebrows waggled up and down, and TJ squirmed in his chair.

"No. I suppose it was the soup and bread, nothing more. She didn't seem to have much, but she was happy to share." The air crackled with Redford's implication. Well, TJ would set that straight right here and now. "And that's all there was to it."

They both stared as the trim figure of Mrs. Rycroft slipped across the street, the feathers on her blue bonnet bobbing with each step. Was that twinkle still in the sheriff's eye? Didn't that beat all? He could lose it right now. TJ O'Brien had absolutely no intention of being strapped to a widow, beautiful or not. Freedom, solitude. Goals he intended to keep hold of with both hands.

"Zach." Sarah Anne called her son to keep up with her. He'd found a great hiding place behind the water barrel in front of the saloon. "Come along, now, Zach. Stay by Mama." One of the patrons could come stumbling out at any minute, and she didn't want Zach subjected to that kind of behavior in a man.

"I hiding from that kitty."

A cat with large ears and a long tail swished around his legs. He giggled, and Sarah broached a smile. Zach dearly wanted a cat, but didn't they have enough pets to care for? Of course, a good barn cat earned its keep soon enough with very little effort. She'd have a talk with Mrs. Haley and see if her cat had any more kittens. Cats were scarce as hen's teeth in Gullywash, but she'd try.

Sarah sidestepped a fresh and smelly pile of horse

manure, pinching her nose and motioning for Zach to jump over the mess.

Her feet tapped a steady rhythm once she stepped onto the boardwalk in front of Haleys' General Store. Looking up from cleaning the entrance, Mrs. Haley startled. Sarah smiled at the stout woman, who diligently swept into each of the corners as if the patrons might comment on her cleanliness. She placed a hand over her heart. "Lands, but you surprised me, Miz Rycroft. Mornin' to you. Fair day in spite of the smattering of clouds earlier." She looked at Zach. "And you, young man. Mornin' to you, too."

Sarah raised her brow at her son. "What do you say, Zachary?"

"Mornin'. What's a smatter?" Then he skipped off in search of the kitty, who'd entered Haleys'. Mrs. Haley laughed.

Sarah loved that boy, but she had business to conduct. "Mrs. Haley. Look. I have two dozen eggs and some butter."

The storekeeper's eyes lit up. "A few double yolks, I hope. You have the largest eggs, I swan. The finest around. I can tell by how they fit in my hand." She smiled. "Yours are always the heaviest, too. Oh, yes, indeed. And with bright yellow yolks."

"Well, I don't skimp on the hens' feed. I pepper good and strong so my hens stay healthy. They work hard for me—the least I can do is feed them proper. I suppose that does make the difference."

Mrs. Haley moved aside, inviting Sarah to enter the store. "Come right on along and let me have a look."

With a glance ahead, Sarah observed Zach already in the front, having forgotten the kitty in order to give his attention to the horehound candy sticks in the glass jar. She liked the peppermint ones best, but she wasn't about to waste money on herself. And even though he knew better than to ask for sweets, her son's eyes said, *Please, Mama. Just one?* She winked at Mrs. Haley, who would sneak a stick into the packages before they left, as always.

Sarah gave Mrs. Haley the basket of eggs and butter, then walked the sides of the store checking for any items she might need and had forgotten to put on her list.

Mrs. Haley gasped. "Lands! You have at least three pounds of butter here. My, the restaurant will be happy to see this."

Sarah strolled back to the front. "I'm glad Mr. Harkins likes it."

Mrs. Haley leaned in and whispered, "I won't admit to sayin' so, but he told me he only likes your butter. Says the other ladies don't salt theirs near enough. And I can tell you color yours. It looks like a ray of sunshine. He pays me ten cents a pound more for your butter." She smirked and pulled a face. "I don't s'pose I ought to tell you that. You'll be making bargains with the man himself."

"A little carrot juice goes a long way when the butter's pale," Sarah replied. "And you've always done right by me by letting me barter. I'll bring my butter to no one but you. Can't you just see me trading my butter for a Sunday dinner? How wasteful that would be when I can barter for goods I need in here."

"Well, then…" The shopkeeper laughed. "Your secret's fine with me. And don't worry—we'll be taking good care of you with your purchases."

"You always do, Mrs.—"

"Ladies." A man's deep voice broke the air.

Sarah turned from her now-empty basket. Sheriff Redford nodded as he and a taller man stepped inside. "Mrs. Haley, I don't believe you've met our new preacher here." The other man slid his hat from his head.

Sarah's face warmed. The man who'd saved her son. She noticed again how very handsome he was. No more half a day's beard on his face, only a clean strong-set jaw and those piercing gray… No…blue… No…gray eyes. Well, she couldn't tell for certain. She put that thought away. No room or time for men in her life. Her wedding ring shone on her finger. Her thoughts were disloyal to Nathaniel's memory, and besides, TJ was a preacher. The last kind of man she'd want anything to do with. *If* she were interested, which she wasn't.

She tried to look away but found her gaze resting on his strong jaw again. A man of some stature even without his hat on.

"Nice to meet you, Mrs. Haley." Then the preacher's words covered Sarah like a soft, warm quilt. "Why, Mrs. Rycroft, isn't it?" He extended his hand, and she shuddered against the strong grip that came with a heart-stopping warmth. She noticed his dimples as he smiled. "Good to see you again." Then he ruffled the curly brown hair on Zach's head. "Stayin' off the roof, I hope, young fella." His smile lit the room, and Sarah had to look away or humiliate herself by gawking.

"Yes, sir. Mama had *a talk* with me. And after talks, I a'member to listen."

The preacher's eyebrows rose with interest. "What kind of *talks,* Zach?"

"Mama calls 'em hand-to-fanny com…ber…stations."

He giggled, trying to say the word, and everyone else in the room grinned, all but Sarah. She'd had a hard time smiling since Nathaniel's death and was out of practice.

TJ dropped to one knee and drew Zach to him. "My uncle had some hand-to-fanny conversations with me, too, when I was growing up. Do you know what else my uncle used to do?"

Big eyes questioned him. "What?"

"If I was being really good and didn't need the hand on my britches—really good, mind you—he'd once in a while get me a treat for working so hard at my manners."

"He did?" Zach's mouth dropped open and he leaned in to whisper, "What kinda treat?"

The preacher threw his head back and laughed. "Why, a horehound stick, of course." Then he looked up at Sarah and winked. "Do you think Zach has been that good since I caught him falling off your roof?"

The sheriff's eyebrow rose and Mrs. Haley put a hand over her heart for the second time that day. "Lands! The boy fell off your roof? Why, how'd he ever climb up there? He's too little for escapades like that." Sarah could almost hear the patter of Mrs. Haley's heart beating in her chest. Poor soul.

Zach smiled wide. "I climbeded the tree and walked on the roof. It was easy for a big boy." He plucked a thumb toward his chest and appeared every bit his father. Sarah choked back an unexpected hitch in her own chest.

With a stern look that must have had a lot of practice quieting rowdy Sunday school students at some time, the preacher stared at Zach. "But not again, right, young fella?"

His little head shook side to side in all sincerity. "No, sir. Not again."

The preacher patted Zach's shoulder and glanced at the candy counter. He held up two fingers to Mrs. Haley. As he stood, the clean sent of pine soap filled Sarah's nostrils. She gazed about to see if Mrs. Haley had put any out. But, as she'd thought, the wonderful aroma came from the preacher. Whether he was handsome and sweet smelling or not, it was Sarah's job to provide for her son. "That's not necessary."

He glanced her way and grinned. "Neither was taking in a stranger for dinner, but you and your son did just that the day I rode in thirsty and hungry, and I appreciated it. Let me return the favor by getting a candy for your son."

"All right." She absolutely hated being indebted to someone, especially a preacher, of all people. Though it irritated the ticks off her, she had to remember her manners. "Thank you, Mr. O'Brien."

She also hated the way her mind swirled with unanswered possibilities.

TJ frowned. So she could give but not receive graciously. He leaned down with the small paper sack in hand. "Zach, only when your mama says it's all right to have the candy. You have to wait. It's good to learn self-discipline. Do you understand?"

"Yes, sir. Thank you, Mis-ter…?"

"O'Brien."

"Thank you, Mis-ter O'Brien." As the boy worked hard to say his name correctly, he held out his hand in a manly fashion. TJ shook it and chuckled at the way

Zach tried to squeeze hard. He could almost envision the older Rycroft male before he had passed on.

Sarah added, "Yes, thank you very much." But he could see it galled her to accept a kindness. She bent toward her son. "Not until after lunch, Zach."

Obviously flustered, she rushed through her purchases and didn't give him another glance, which suited him fine. He was on his way to Harkins' for dinner anyway. The restaurant owner provided his dinners in town, and TJ ate breakfast and supper at the sheriff's house. He'd rotate homes when he came back each month unless the sheriff offered the room each time, but Mr. Harkins at the restaurant insisted he should have dinner with them whenever he wanted. Who was he to argue? The restaurant's dried-apple pie tasted like heaven. Harkins was a lucky man indeed to have a wife who cooked so well. Did every woman turn into a wonderful cook as soon as she made her way west? Because so far he hadn't eaten a truly bad meal.

He tipped his hat to the ladies, his gaze lingering over Sarah, then turned to Redford. "See you later, Sheriff."

"You're welcome to the back office to work on your sermons, if you're so inclined."

TJ spun on his heel and with a hearty laugh said, "Exactly where I need to put together a sermon. In your jail. Might help to meditate on sin, though."

"Well—" Redford laughed "—you are planning on using the saloon for Sunday service. This way you can preach to 'em before and after jail."

"Thanks anyway, but the good outdoors provides the best lessons in God's handiwork. I'll see you before supper. My best to your wife for that fine breakfast."

His boots stirred the dust in the road as a huge yellow cat whizzed past him. An old stray mongrel missing a back leg followed right behind the best he could, teeth snapping the air barely inches from the cat's tail, and TJ secretly cheered for the dog to catch up. Ten more steps and he was inside Harkins' Good Food.

"Hey, Mr. Harkins. I'm here to impose on your fine offer one more time."

A short balding man with big ears and a strong accent rushed to his side. Food spattered the apron he had tied around his neck. "No, no. Nefer imposing. You velcome anytime, preacher man."

"Well, then. I guess you know what I'll be having. A beef biscuit and apple p—"

"Not today. No *Apfel* pie." Through the window, the sun shone off his shaking head, but he winked. "No. Today, Mama, she make strudel. You like *Apfel* pie, you'll like strudel efen more."

"Well, then. A beef biscuit and apple strudel."

Once Mr. Harkins headed for the kitchen, TJ noticed Zach at the front window, staring in and licking his lips. How well did they get on anyway? Sarah had said they had plenty to eat. Had she been telling the truth?

Chapter 3

"Not today, little man." Sarah plucked Zach from the front of Harkins' restaurant and looked in the window. Inside was the preacher, and he was gazing at them. She pushed Zach's backside toward their wagon. Anything to get away from those eyes that seemed to draw her in, call her name, question her intentions of staying away. "We'll head home and I'll fix your dinner. How about a big bowl of corn pudding with maple syrup drizzled on top?"

"Oooh, I like corn puddin', Mama."

She couldn't resist one look over her shoulder at the preacher in the window and then turned and planted a kiss on Zach's head. "I know. That's why I left a pot simmering on the stove before we started out this morning." Of course, the preacher had every right to eat in Harkins'. No doubt staring out the window at the passersby. As anyone else would do. Nothing more, nothing less. It had merely been a coincidence that she'd been the one walking past.

Sarah loaded Zach into the back of the wagon so he could play on the way home. And while he was preoccupied opening the leather pouch that held his marbles, she tucked a canvas bag into the front of the wagon bed. Wouldn't he be surprised, though.

"Zach. You might want to open that bag."

"How come, Mama?"

"Well, you ought to let Sassy out."

"Sassy?" He immediately stopped playing with his marbles and pulled the bag open. "A kitty!" he cried. "Is it for me?"

"Yes, and make sure to hang on to her." His joy became her own. "She's for our barn. But you can take care of her and play with her when she's not busy catching mice."

"You mean mouses?"

Sarah kept the brake in place and turned to rub the soft fur held snugly in Zach's arms. "Yes, she'll catch mice once she's big enough, but we'll still give her a dish of fresh milk each day and scraps from the table. But not too much. She needs to hunt to be happy. This is one of Sunshine's kittens. You remember the yellow kitty that chased you today?"

"That's her mama?"

"Yes, son. But now you'll take care of her instead of her mama. She belongs to you and if you take good care of her, she'll always stay with you."

His wide eyes searched her face. "Didn't you take good care of Papa?"

"What?" Her stomach pressed bile into her throat.

"He didn't stay, did he? So you didn't take good care of him?"

Sarah fought tears and turned back to the wagon seat, swallowing down the burning acid while sheltering herself with her own arms. They didn't comfort the way Nathaniel's used to. "It's not the same, Zach." She glanced back at her son cuddling the kitten. Then she looked down the street, saw folks strolling along oblivious to her pain. The world spun around her and no one knew. No one saw how she hurt. Like a raw wound open to the air. Would it ever heal? Ever stop hurting?

Zach cuddled Sassy in his arms and buried his face in the soft fur.

"Just you be careful until she's used to you. She has sharp claws even though she's a kitten, and I don't want you hurt." There hadn't been words to explain Nathaniel's death. At least, it didn't appear she'd done a good job of making clear what had happened.

"I know, Mama. I'm not a baby anymore."

"Yes, yes. I know." She swiped a tear away. "You aren't a baby anymore."

TJ continued to stare out the window, taking in the scene of a mother with her child. So she'd given the boy a kitten. One more animal for her to take care of on that big farm. Her love for the little boy had to be great indeed to add more chores to her daily list, but that was apparently the way of parents. He couldn't know for sure, though his uncle had been wonderful—what TJ thought a father should be.

Sarah crumpled forward on the wagon seat, holding her sides against what? Pain? TJ stood. Did she need help? He paused, deciding to wait a few minutes to see what happened. She straightened and slapped the reins; then she and the boy took off down the road. An empty black hole grew in his chest. A hole only a smile from Sarah would fill.

Mr. Harkins arrived with his food and TJ stopped watching the wagon as it grew smaller along the road. Now he attempted to have eyes only for the wonderful meal, but the thought of Sarah's eyes, browner and warmer than his coffee, kept invading his vision. Nonsense!

He placed a napkin on his lap. Ahh, yes. Hot coffee, biscuits stuffed with thin slices of sweet ginger-flavored roast beef and apple strudel. He lifted a flaky edge of crust from the plate to his lips and tasted the buttery goodness. Mr. Harkins was right. Apple strudel beat apple pie hands down.

"Hey, there, TJ."

"Well, long time no see, Sheriff. Pull up a chair. Thought I'd grab a bite before I started on my sermon. You ever had this strudel stuff before?"

"Harkins introduced me to strudel three years ago when he and his wife first came to town. You can't beat Wanda Harkins's cooking. But don't tell my wife, Molly, I said that."

He took in the sheriff's ample frame in an exaggerated manner. "Seems to me you must like her cooking right enough, too. Appears she feeds you fairly well."

The sheriff laughed out loud and hugged his sides. "That she does. A bit too well."

TJ smiled. "Well, your secret's good with me. Say, I noticed Mrs. Rycroft with a kitten for her son." The boy's grin had been ear to ear when he'd cuddled the animal in his lap. TJ wished he could see a smile like that on the mother's face. He wasn't sure he'd seen her smile once since he'd met her. As a man who hadn't even kissed a woman before, he found it difficult to imagine the kind of closeness a man and his wife must feel for each other. And yet he tried to preach to them as if he understood. Well, he had scripture to go by. But did that count? Only reading about relationships? The best relationship he'd ever had in his life had been with his uncle. Uncle Michael had meant the world to him, and he was grateful for their time together, but TJ had kept his distance from women. All he wanted in life was his relationship with Christ and his freedom. His ability to come and go. That *was* all he wanted, right?

"Yes, well," the sheriff said, interrupting TJ's thoughts, "the way I understand it after talking to Mrs. Haley, Sarah is afraid the farm could be taken from them and she wants the boy to have something of his own for when they move. Make it easier, you know?" He glanced over at the owner and waved for a cup of coffee. "The little guy has had a hard time of it, losing his father, and now his mother scraping to get by."

TJ set his cup down to let it cool. "Things are that bad for her and the boy? Looked like a decent sort of farm. Can hardly believe a woman and small boy could care for a farm like that and do such a fine job of it. How does she?" Shouldn't have asked. Asking brings answers that cause problems, and he didn't need any problems. He was happy. He was free, coming and going as he pleased. Then why this sudden ache in the pit of his belly? Not the strudel's fault, that much he knew for sure.

Sheriff Redford finally took a seat as Harkins brought his coffee. "Because it's a workin' farm, they have plenty to eat, but if she brought in a decent amount of wheat this year, I think she'd be all right. And yet I have to ask myself, how much can a woman and small boy do to reap a profitable crop? I don't know. She managed last year, but she sold a fine string of horses Nathaniel had raised, as well. And for a mighty pretty penny. At least, enough to please old Banker Studdard. Still, the balance all comes due this autumn. I know she's being mighty careful about spending. She trades her eggs and butter for groceries."

TJ shook his head, ran fingers through his hair. "Doesn't she have any help?"

"James Studdard, the banker's oldest son, comes out in the spring and plows, but Sarah Anne and the boy put the seeds in. She paid James cash last year, but this year I hear she offered him the pick of the piglets as part of the payment. I think Studdard allows the boy to do it more to keep an eye on the farm than as any type of charity. He's not convinced a woman can run it properly. For such a respected member of the community, he can be a rascal. I'm figurin' if he had his way, he'd put her out the first chance he got." He shook his head. "I'm sure I've seen him wringing his hands when he locks eyes with greenbacks."

Put her out? What kind of man did that? "Any chance he has another buyer for the property? That would account for his interest in how well she does."

The sheriff rubbed his chin. "Didn't think about that. S'pose it could be. He's a shrewd businessman, our banker. Always has been. Can't fault him for making the money he deserves, but if that's the case, then there's no way he'll allow his boy to help bring in the wheat. He'll want her to fail. He'll need for her to fail in order to pay off the note himself and then turn it around to a buyer. I'm thinkin' you might be onto something." Redford downed his coffee in two gulps. The man sure loved his coffee. "I might do a bit of askin' around. I hope we're wrong. I'd hate to think a church-going man could be that heartless to a widow lady and her little boy."

A widow lady. That expression brought up the image of an older woman, a shawl wrapped over her head and silver curls peeking out. That most assuredly was not Sarah Anne Rycroft. He chuckled, remembering her standing at the door with a rifle nearly as heavy as she, aimed straight at his heart. Now she aimed those sad eyes at his heart instead. TJ shook his head. Where were those thoughts coming from? And why?

The sheriff smiled. "What's funny about that?"

TJ gulped down the last bite of strudel, as if shoveling in food would remove the sappy look from his face. "I was thinking how Sarah Anne would feel knowing we were talking about her as if she were a helpless widow lady. I doubt she'd cotton to it much."

Redford rose and slapped him on the shoulder. "I think you're right. She wouldn't take to it one bit. That's one independent lady."

Tuesday morning, Sarah had finally pried Sassy out of Zach's hands and settled the kitten onto a bed of straw on the front porch. Zach scampered about the house searching for an old rag to add to the box. "To cover her," he'd said. Her heart tripped over itself enjoying the way he cared for others. Like his father all the way. Would she ever get over losing Nathaniel when she saw his face every single day in Zach?

A chest-rattling sigh burst from her lips. Maybe...

and maybe not. It was getting more difficult to see his face in her mind—only when she looked at her son... there he was, plain as day.

Light footsteps padded over the floor. "Here's a blanket, Mama. For Sassy." He held a piece of old rag in his fingers like a prized possession.

"Where'd you get that, Zach?"

"The rag bag. You said I could, a'member?"

"I do now." She took the soft piece of gray wool that had been part of a blanket she and Nathaniel had been given when they married. She snuggled it around Sassy, not convinced the kitten was very happy about her new bedding, but eventually, Sassy kneaded it for a few minutes and settled down to sleep. "Zach, did you give her the warm milk?"

"Yes, ma'am. She licked the bowl clean."

"Well, it will be your job to wash the dish out and put fresh water in it each day after she has her milk. Can you do that? And always use the same bowl. That one is for no one else but her to use."

He planted hands on his hips and did his best to raise a brow the way his father used to. "I'm big. I can take care of Sassy. I'll even help her catch mouses."

"Mice," Sarah corrected, hiding her grin. "I'm not sure she'll need your help catching the mice, but if you keep her dish very clean, she'll be happy and she will catch all the mice that come into our barn."

Sassy licked her paws and washed the milk from her face. Zach's gaze didn't leave her for a second, but Sarah glanced up at the sound of hoofbeats. She peeked around the curtain rather than running for the rifle as she would have before. She wasn't sure why, but since meeting TJ, she had grown more confident.

The preacher's big bay trotted right up to the front. What was TJ still doing in town? Or had he said he'd be staying until Tuesday? She couldn't rightly remember, but he should leave. She didn't like the way his eyes reached into her soul and saw feelings where no one else was allowed. Or the way her heart fluttered in her chest whenever he came near. That had to stop. Those flutters and a penny could buy her a heap of trouble.

Sarah opened the door and stood on the porch. Zach ran out from behind her, Sassy in his arms.

TJ rode past the well this time and stopped at the porch. After waving a quick salute, he dismounted with ease, tossed the bridle over the porch rail and addressed her son as if he'd known him forever. Almost as though he belonged there, and that kind of familiarity had to stop. Two sticks of candy didn't entitle him to think he belonged.

His gaze scanned the scene. "What have you got there, Zach Rycroft?"

Two little hands grasped the kitten and held her aloft. "A kitty. Her nameses Sassy. Wanna pet her?"

The raven-haired preacher reached for the kitten, who was quickly swallowed up in the man's big hands. "Well, will you look at this sweet little girl." He flipped her onto her back and cradled her in his arm as he stroked her soft belly. Her purr stuttered, stopped and started again, as kittens were wont to do. And she didn't move a bit, content in his comforting hands.

Sarah shook her head and straightened. Nonsense and feathers.

"Listen. Her's happy." Zach pointed at the cuddled kitten.

Sarah couldn't stifle the smile in spite of her best intentions. Here was this giant of a man draped in a long black coat, and a wee kitten lay hidden in his arm. "Is she still in there?"

Her smile must have been contagious. The preacher chuckled all the way to his blue-gray eyes as he handed Sassy back to Zach. "Make her feel warm and safe, young man, and she'll love you forever." Laugh lines fanned across his face. Too many for one so young. Where *had* he come from? And why did the solitary life seem to please him?

Sarah bit her lip. All questions she did not need answers for. She had her life; he had his. Both alone. Both happy that way.

Zach looked up full of wonder as the kitten curled against his shoulder. "She loves me forever?"

Forever. Or until she dies unexpectedly. Sarah's face physically fell and she reached for the porch rail to keep herself from collapsing. "Pardon me. I believe I need to sit down."

The preacher leaped up the steps and took her in his arms. "Sit on this stool." He pulled the small wooden bench closer with his foot. "Sarah. Sit down before you fall."

"I'm sorry, Nathaniel. I felt faint for a second." No! Nathaniel was gone. This was the preacher. She fought the black spots in her eyes as her legs slipped out from under her.

"Sarah. Sarah!"

"Thank you for the wet cloth, Zach," Sarah mumbled. "It's hot today, is all. Your mama will be fine."

TJ wiped her face with the cool rag, and he could smell the lavender on her skin. "Sarah?" he asked softly. "You all right?" Had to keep his mind on helping, not on how wonderful she smelled, but some things got in the way and couldn't be helped. Like the soft feel of her face under his hand. He'd never thought about how soft a woman's skin was. Not until now.

Her eyes flickered for a second, and then a frown appeared to let him know she didn't understand what had happened. "What? Where am I? Where's Zachary?"

"We're all on the porch. You were simply overheated. Zach's right here by me."

"Oh." She fought to sit up, and he continued to cradle her as he had the kitten. But like kittens, a frightened woman could scratch. She struggled against his best efforts to calm her. He'd better let her up. As she rose from his grasp to sit by herself, the lavender filled his senses again, and he fought to think of *any* single thing other than the fact she was a mighty pretty, sweet-smelling, soft-feeling woman.

The frown on her face frightened him. No one should appear that lost, that lonely, that afraid.

What could he do to bring back her beautiful smile? As suddenly as it had appeared, it had disappeared when she'd fainted. Why? He shook his head. Didn't really matter. He'd fill his canteen, and once he knew she was all right, he'd move on out of town. Then no more worries about the widow and her son for another month.

"Do you think you can stand up?" he asked.

She brushed at the front of her skirt as if that gave him his answer. "Of course I can. You're right. It was just the heat bearing down. I've been canning. Too hot in the kitchen, I guess."

"Mama, you looked funny. And you dinnunt hear me call you."

She waved Zach's comment aside with a grin, which

she obviously forced for her boy's sake. "I'm fine now, son."

TJ took her words and facial expression to mean she was dismissing him, as well. "Do you mind if I fill my canteen before I go?"

"Not at all." Her teeth worked the edge of her lip as he'd seen her do before when she appeared to be miles away. "Headed on to the next town?"

He nodded but didn't move. With his gaze locked on to those almond-shaped brown eyes, his feet rooted themselves to the porch. *Dear Lord, what can I do for these two? I feel so helpless. Is it safe for me to leave? They should have someone looking over them every day.*

"Yes, the good folks expect me to arrive by Thursday. I actually have a wedding next weekend. And if Mr. Merriman isn't doing better when I arrive, there might be a funeral, as well."

"A wedding." Her face registered more sadness than he could deal with. "And a funeral. I'm sorry. For the funeral, I mean."

"I'm the one who's sorry. I've put my very large foot into my mouth. Sarah, if I haven't said it well enough before now, I am truly sorry for your loss." He reached out, touched a curl and drew his hand away much as if her blond hair had been on fire. Thinking she might faint again, he waited. "I wish I had words of comfort for you, but I don't. I haven't ever experienced the kind of loss you have." Losing parents couldn't be the same as losing a husband.

Saul nickered next to them and reminded him why he'd stopped. "Maybe I should be going."

"Mis-ter O'Brien. Don't go. Can't you stay and play with me and Sassy?"

Sarah answered without hesitating, "He has to go, sweetie. He preaches in another town this week."

TJ knelt to the ground. "How about if when I come back in a month, we'll make Sassy her own crate for the porch here? I'll show you how to cut the wood for a little house." He glanced in Sarah's direction. "If it's all right with your mama, that is."

Zach's face lit up like a jar of fireflies. "Well? Is it, Mama?"

The pink in her cheeks again and the return of Sarah's smile told him he'd be welcome anytime. "Let me serve you a meal before you head out, Preacher. Please. It's the least I can do for all the kind things you've done for Zach. And me. You always seem to be coming to our rescue."

Well, that was what a preacher did. Not just for beautiful, young widow ladies but for all his flock. "I don't want to put you out." His face creased into a grin. "Though I wouldn't want to insult your kindness, either." He breathed appreciatively of the delicious scent wafting through the open door and gazed again at the pale yellow curls surrounding her face and remembered how like silk they had felt for that brief moment. No, he wouldn't mind at all.

"You won't be. I put a pot of beans and molasses on this morning before I started the chores. With some fresh bread and honey—"

"They'll be a welcome treat. Thank you."

With an odd sense of loneliness she hadn't felt in the past couple of years, Sarah watched and listened until she couldn't hear the clopping of hoofbeats any longer. While she didn't really care one way or the other, it had been nice when someone had paid attention to Zach. Especially a man who could teach him all the things she couldn't. A handsome man with black hair and caring eyes. A man who could… *No. Stop this, Sarah. Right now.* She did not need another man in her life or in Zach's. They had lost the most wonderful man God had created. God? Well, sure. He had created Nathaniel, but then He had taken him away. What kind of God did that to folks?

An uncaring God. A God who had brought them into a land with no other family and then deserted Sarah and Zach. Took away the only good man she had ever known other than her pa. The one who first kissed her on her sixteenth birthday. She lifted fingers to her lips, trying to feel the warmth and sweetness of that very first kiss. The memory overwhelmed her. He had loved her, cared enough to put her before his own comforts. And then he went…first. *Why, God? Why did You destroy our lives like this? Me without my precious husband and Zach without his father?*

Sarah dashed into the house, slamming the door and leaving her son on the porch with the kitten. She tore into the back bedroom and threw herself across the bed, where tears exhausted her sense of worth for half an hour.

Chapter 4

The batting eyes of Jeanette Loiller trapped him. TJ swallowed hard and did his best to avoid her obvious attempts at flirtation. Sitting at the Loillers' comfortable kitchen table, eggs and bacon teasing his taste buds, he leaned back in his chair and drew deep of the smell of the delicious coffee that Jeanette's mother had placed in front of him. The room gave off charm and warmth. Curtains with little curlicue things cut out along the edges let in just enough sun that the room had light most of the day. He'd stayed with them before, and always they made him feel very much at home.

Until today.

For some reason, Mrs. Loiller and her daughter had decided a single preacher must be lonely. He dipped his head, avoiding the mother's stares and the daughter's wide-eyed adoration, and instead addressed the food in front of him. When he did finally glance up, Jeanette's eyes locked on to his…again.

She gazed longingly at him, lids fluttering like butterflies. Butterflies he could tolerate. Jeanette? No thank you very much. He hadn't given her reason to think he had an interest in her. But staying with her family while in town, he couldn't very well *go home*. This was home. He smiled and nodded at the story she told, all the while pulling his watch from his pocket time and again, praying she and her mama would get the hint. "It's getting late. And I have preparations to make for my sermon."

Mrs. Loiller pushed Jeanette aside. "Don't go, Preacher. I've got more bacon and coffee. You do like your coffee. I've been paying attention." Her eager face sparkled, and he gulped back what he'd have liked to say. She'd been paying far too much attention to his business.

Once he finished breakfast, he'd head for school, where they held services, preach his sermon and pack up so he could leave first thing tomorrow morning. The Schoenherrs had invited him for dinner, which offered him refuge during that meal. One more day with Mrs. Loiller, and she'd have him and Jeanette engaged. At supper he would nod kindly at their stories and excuse himself early for bed before the two women sank their claws in again.

Who was he kidding? His irritation wasn't with these lovely folks; it stemmed from the fact that he'd thought of no one but Mrs. Rycroft since he'd been in Gullywash. Now he'd leave Paceoff and head to Lost Cap, then Tideville and finally back to Gullywash. A perfect diamond-shaped route. A diamond. A jewel. Sarah Anne was a jewel, all right.

"Mr. O'Brien." Flutter…flutter…flutter. "You seem miles away from here. Are you so anxious to leave us this soon?" Mrs. Loiller's hand lingered close to his on the table and he drew back. "Gracious, but we love having you here with us, don't we, Jeanette? Makes us feel as if we're doing our part, you know, housing the preacher and all. It's our pleasure, don'tcha know?"

"No, I, uh, well… I have my sermon on my mind. Always planning the next one and such. You understand. A preacher's life is very dull." He leveled a withered stare in her direction. "Dry old sermons and heavy topics take a great deal of research and study. Folks wanting you every second so they can tell you their sorrows take up what little time is left over. Never a full night's sleep. Always moving town to town. Yes, quite an uncomfortable, boring life."

Mrs. Loiller's lips pursed into a straight dry line. "My, I didn't think about that." She pulled her fingers back and sat straighter in her seat. "When you put it that way…" Her eyes had lost their sparkle. Maybe having a preacher for a son-in-law wasn't such a prize after all.

"Oh, yes. A dull life with no time for anyone or anything but the Gospel." In truth, that was what he'd planned for his life all along, but he'd found it not as time-consuming as he'd originally believed.

Jeanette swallowed her last bite and spoke up. "My, but you don't seem to be like that at all." Still, her mouth turned down at the edges for the first time since he'd arrived. It was good to know she frowned on occasion; all he'd seen for days was that forced smile hanging on her face like a cheap strip of wallpaper without enough glue. Not like...

"Well, you see—"

"Why, you've always been the first to tell a funny story and to help with dishes. You've been so kind to me...all of us. Everyone in town. And now you make it sound like it's such a chore." Her fingers twisted the napkin in her lap.

TJ quirked what he knew would be a patronizing smile. "If I did, I apologize, Jeanette. This town is filled with very friendly folks and it's easy to forget myself at times. Perhaps I'm saying too much, but you all make me feel at home. I guess folks now and then think traveling preachers are carefree. Nothing to hold them down, but it's almost the opposite. Still, your family is overly generous to me when I'm in town, and I have no right to complain." Was he lying to her? Or to himself? No, not since he'd met Sarah Anne. He was tied down, all right. She had a cord twisted around his heart and connected across the miles to hers. She was the only thing he thought about. And that had to stop.

Sarah stopped her mind wandering as she swept dry crumbs from the table and noticed her son dawdling. "Zach, finish your milk before you go tend to the kitty." If that preacher were here, he'd see to it Zach minded. Why was it so difficult for her?

That preacher. The big man with laughing eyes and a smile to warm any heart.

She gasped. She'd been thinking of another man. And fondly. She couldn't; she just couldn't—wouldn't.

Zach slumped in his chair, all his four-year-old joy gone in an instant. "But Maa-ma."

"Sassy will still be waiting for you. You need to drink your milk to grow big and strong the same way Sassy does." Sarah rose from her seat and poured some more in a cup. "When you finish, you can take this out and put it in Sassy's dish right proper. Then don't forget—"

"To clean the dish and gets clean water for her. I a'member."

I a'member. Gazing into his eyes, she thought of when she and Nathaniel had put the last floorboard into their house. He'd gone to the barn and pulled the wagon around, asked her for a list of provisions they'd need and then handed her back the list after he'd had a look.

But you'll forget what we need.

I'll a'member.

When he'd returned, he'd had all the packages balanced in his arms. *Take the top one first.* Pokes and bumps had filled the brown paper, and she couldn't imagine what he'd bought. Probably a new toy for their baby.

She'd dug into the package as if it were Christmas morning. A kerosene lamp. Flowers and vines twined all around the base and the clear glass top shone, sparkling and clean. *It's beautiful. But you didn't have to spend money on me.*

Yes, I did. And then he'd kissed her.

He had remembered all the items on her list. And a lamp.

The lamp still filled the corner of the room with a soft glow at night as well as with memories. Whenever she lit it, her heart broke thinking of the day he had given her the precious gift.

Sarah sighed. When might it be time enough to move

on? For two years she'd cried herself to sleep more often than she wanted to remember. Nathaniel filled every nook and cranny of this house. His handiwork dwelled along each board and each corner of her heart. *How long, God? How long before You start loving me again enough to let me have my life back?*

Jeanette Loiller picked a wild rose from the front of the porch and sniffed it, smiling. Then she slipped it into TJ's pocket. Startled, he tossed the reins over Saul's head as fast as he could. His saddlebag and bedroll attached and ready for him to leave, he guided Saul from the Loillers' property, Jeanette still waving a hankie. Without another look back, he eased into the rhythm Saul set. Past the sweet scent of the wild roses, crossing the deep wagon ruts in the road, over the shallow creek bed, he swayed on Saul's back. Once TJ had cleared the town proper, he clicked his tongue, and the bay settled into a comfortable trot. A breeze streamed over TJ's face and under his collar. He couldn't get away fast enough. Jeanette had bought his sad story for only so long and then the lashes had begun their fluttering all over again. And the mother. Could no man be single and happy? Mrs. Loiller's words, *Come back soon. We are always very happy to see you, aren't we, Jeanette?* haunted him in spite of his escape. There had to be a different family that he could stay with. A family without a daughter coming of age. Or with a mother satisfied to have her daughter married to the owner of the restaurant, or any single man but TJ. He'd be right proud to preside over the marriage ceremony for the happy couple, but let him be.

With a sharp move, he reached over and patted Saul

on the neck. "Let's go, fella. Get away from the femi-
nine wiles. It's you and me again on the open road. Two
more weeks. We'll be back in Gullywash and then…"
And then TJ would have to deal with a different kind
of femininity. Sarah Anne Rycroft. Her pain-filled
eyes tormented his sense of decency. What or who had
turned her away from God? That was a foolish notion.
He knew the answer. The death of her husband.

TJ prided himself on helping others while keeping
his distance. But Sarah had built walls… Walls that sur-
rounded her and the boy like a fortress. And could TJ,
like Joshua, march around her disillusionment seven
times and bring down the walls? His job required him
to try. That was all. No other reason. Just march right
up to her and say, "Sarah Anne, God loves you. You
need to turn back to God."

All right, so that probably wouldn't move even the
smallest mountain. What, then? What would turn her
back to her faith? Whatever might help, he didn't have
a clue. And he shouldn't dwell on her problems anyway.
There were other folks who needed him.

But none who held his heart in their hands.

He stroked Saul's mane again. "Well, boy, we have
our work cut out for us. We have to find a way in the
next two weeks to figure out how to convince Mrs.
Rycroft that God loves her. Think we can do it?" He
groaned. "Think we can do it without being trapped?"

Saul reared back and turned his head. His teeth came
dangerously close to nipping TJ's hand. "That was not
the confident response I was hoping for, fella."

The heads of wheat were nearly in their milk. Sarah
walked the field and allowed her fingers to ruffle the

thick green crop. Not quite ready yet, but the wheat grew strong and tall, the tops heavy with hope. A few more weeks and she'd be able to harvest a bountiful crop. Enough to pay off the banknote a few weeks earlier than expected. For a moment she convinced herself she heard God talking to her heart, telling her to trust once again. But that couldn't be.

Tears that had bottled behind her eyes for two years where God was concerned dribbled at first, then scorched her cheeks with hot moisture. *Is that it? Did You simply want me to trust You again? All right. I'll try. Give me a chance and I'll try. Look at this wheat, Lord. If this is the answer, I thank You for helping me and Zach.*

With what she recognized as a bounce in her step, Sarah whirled around like a child, letting the aroma of growing wheat and manure fill her nostrils. *My crop! I'll be able to pay off the note and get Zach new shoes for winter. I'll prove I was able to do it to Banker Studdard. And the rest of the town. My crop...my farm. And I did it! All by myself.*

"Mama, what's you laughin' at?"

Without a care, she dropped to her knees in the soil. "I'm happy, Zach. For the first time in a very long time, your mama's really happy."

"I'm always happy, Mama. And so's Sassy."

Drawing him into her arms, Sarah nuzzled his neck until he pulled back. "All right. I know. You aren't a baby anymore. But I still like to kiss you."

"Well, when nobody's lookin'. All right." And he hugged her around the neck.

"Zach, what would you like when I take our crop to market? Anything you want."

"For you to be happy, Mama. You cry too much."

He'd heard her at night, of that she was certain. "I'm sorry, Zach. Sometimes when I think of your daddy, it makes me sad."

"Mama?"

"Yes."

"I can't a'member what Daddy looked like. I'm sorry."

So much for a child to deal with. Of course he didn't remember Nathaniel. It had been so long ago. Two years to a child... Half his lifetime. "Don't worry, baby. Daddy knows you still love him." Did he know? She stared into her son's hopeful eyes and understood that she had to continue to let him feel he was loved... by her...by Nathaniel.

Today would be a new beginning for her and her precious son. Today she would put God in control again. Because God was blessing her and it was the right thing to do.

A quiver slithered through her stomach, making her pause. It was the dutiful thing, right?

Her fingers fluttered over the stalks of wheat again. Look at this bountiful crop.

Chapter 5

TJ lifted his hat and mopped at the sweat. He thought of the time he'd stopped at Sarah's for a drink. The gun barrel, catching the boy, having dinner with them. He smiled, recalling the little hands grasping for his mother. The tough look he'd tried to level at TJ. Then he laughed outright. Some boy, that little fella. But his mother. The sweet expression when she knew her boy was safe at last. The way she'd wrapped herself around him and cried into his hair. Thanking TJ, when, in fact, the boy wouldn't have been in trouble save for trying to protect his mother. Enough. No more thinking about Sarah.

Hungry and thirsty from riding the dry road that had led him out of Tideville back toward Gullywash, he rode past the Rycroft farm and straight into town. He stopped in front of the sheriff's office and surveyed the area. Drier than usual for this time of year. August brought heat, but right about now, the folks could use some gentle rains to feed the crops and ready them for harvest. Sarah's wheat should be growing thick and healthy by now. Another week and it would be in the milk, ready for her to bring on a work crew and then even up on the note with the bank. Perhaps she'd have a better outlook. Perhaps he'd be able to talk to her about God's love even in times of difficulty. That was, after all, his heart's desire. To bring an understanding of God's love to everyone.

After supper he'd ride out and make good on his promise to Zach. Build a nice crate for the kitten. One that looked like their farmhouse.

"Say, there, young fella."

TJ startled and looked down from Saul's back.

"You here already?" Sheriff Redford planted his legs shoulder width apart, put hands on hips and donned his best tough-guy look. "Not sure Molly's expectin' you till tomorrow."

TJ slid from the saddle. "I can stay at the hotel, Sheriff. I know I'm early. Lady trouble."

"Lady trouble? Here in Gullywash?"

"No, sir." He tied Saul's reins to the hitching post in front of the sheriff's office. "More personal. In Paceoff, and then in Tideville, and sooner or later in Lost Cap with my luck."

"What?"

With a groan that he was sure didn't escape the sheriff's ears, he said, "Sheriff, you have no idea. Every girl and her mama has singled me out for marriage. Like I must be looking for a bride."

Sheriff Redford slapped him on the back. "Come on along, then, and tell me all about it."

"Not much to tell. Just, the family I stayed with last had a mother and daughter who thought every single man should find him a wife. And they both spent each minute I was with them doing their best to pull the preacher in like a bull calf at the end of a rope." He fingered his neck and laughed. "See the noose marks? I had to skedaddle while I was still single. Then in Tideville there is this one single lady who makes no bones about wanting a husband. I might have been a one-legged circus dancer with a blind eye and one ear shot off, and she'd have had me leaning on her to walk down the aisle so's the minister could yell the vows in my good ear. I can't tell you how glad I am to be back in Gullywash."

Redford cracked his knee with the palm of his hand and howled. "Isn't that the truth, boy. Isn't that the truth. Women simply can't stand to see a man happy. I mean, single." He cocked his head sideways and indicated the restaurant across the street. "How about a cup of coffee? And some pie? I seem to remember you like Harkins's apple pie. My treat."

"I wouldn't turn it down, sir. That's a fact. But should I be afraid?"

The sheriff frowned. "Afraid? Of old man Harkins?"

"Well, Mr. Harkins has all daughters. I don't want *him* to be getting any funny ideas if I keep showing up to eat his apple pie. He might think it's just an excuse to spy on his daughters."

When they entered the restaurant, still chuckling over their jokes, Harkins rushed right over. "Ahh, you are back vit us. Nice. Nice. Some *Apfel* strudel?"

"Strudel today?" TJ asked. "Sounds good to me. And nice strong coffee. Black this time."

"Right away." Harkins rushed from the table to the back, laughing as he scurried to fill their order. "Mama, the preacher's back."

"Don't know how that man does it." Sheriff Redford chuckled. "A wife and four daughters to care for."

TJ smiled. "I think that's how. He rushes around barking orders and they do all his bidding. Seems like a fair trade. As long as he doesn't march those girls through here one at a time for me to look over head to toe." He stared toward the back of the restaurant as if half expecting the parade to begin. "I'll tell you, Sheriff, that Loiller woman did everything but tie me up and force me to slip a ring on her daughter's finger. Thought for a minute I was the prize in a rodeo roping." He lowered his voice but spoke like a woman. "Here you go, Preacher. My Jeanette's a *wonderful* cook. A *wonderful* homemaker. A *wonderful* big sister. Going to be a *wonderful* mother someday." He shouldn't poke fun at the anxious woman, but it had been a trying week with them hovering over his every move.

Sheriff Redford held his sides and belly-laughed; TJ had to shush him. "Not so loud, Sheriff. You might give Mrs. Harkins ideas. Why is it a single man *must* be looking for a wife? At least, seems like women all believe that. I'm happy as can be. Me and Saul on the open road. Life without family obligations. Coming and going as I please."

"You don't have to convince me. If it weren't for that beautiful woman who took pity on me years ago, I'd be on that open road with you."

"Took pity? Is that how it works?" TJ asked.

Redford ran a hand through his hair and chuckled. "Well, now. That's how it happened to me. Once I saw that sweet face, all my grand ideas of what I planned to do flew right out'n the window."

Harkins was as good as his word; they had the coffee and strudel in less than a minute. "My oldest daughter, Tildi, she made the *Apfel* strudel fresh today. Such a gut cook." And he winked at TJ as he walked away.

"See there?" TJ smiled. "Now they've got the fellas doing their dirty work. I don't understand. I'm a happy man, Sheriff. Can't I tell them to leave me be?"

"Might as well save your breath." Sheriff Redford grinned and dug into his dessert. "Speaking of unhappy single men..."

"I said happy."

"Six of one, half a dozen of the other. What makes you think Gullywash is safer than your last town?"

"Beg pardon?"

"Listen, I saw Sarah Rycroft in town yesterday. She came to look into a work crew for her harvest."

TJ gulped the next bite of strudel. Was Redford going to pick up where Mrs. Loiller left off?

"Studdard's boy was suddenly taken busy and said he couldn't help her. I expect that is his father's doing. But she found two fellas who would help for a share of the crop. Still, if I know that woman, she'll work herself to death to get the crop in on time doing as much by herself as possible."

A chunk of crust slid down TJ's throat in a dry lump instead of flaky sweetness. First Mrs. Loiller, then Harkins and now the sheriff trying to play matchmaker? Who next?

His gaze roving around the room, anywhere but into

the sheriff's conniving grin, TJ wondered just how long he could fight it before Sarah's problems became his own. In all fairness, she had never asked him for help; in fact, she discouraged him from helping at every turn in the bend. Without thinking, he slammed his hand on the table. "Enough!"

"I'm sorry?" the sheriff asked, his face a mask of confusion. "What did I say riled you, boy?"

TJ shook his head, clearing the cobwebs that filled his mind and caused trouble. "Nothing." He might as well give in. Fighting an overbearing mother was one thing; fighting the sheriff and Sarah was quite impossible.

He could rearrange his schedule and stay in town until the crop came in. Surely another hand who would work for food alone might save her part of the profit. No, he had towns to preach in. Why should he change his entire life to work around Sarah Rycroft's crop?

You could. If you really wanted to. Of course he *could*. But Sarah Anne was not his problem. Was she? She was one of many who needed his attention.

He licked his lips and finished the strudel, but he didn't taste another bite. All of it, like so much sawdust on his tongue, served more to irritate than please him. Still, as he cleaned his plate, alluring eyes and blond hair smiled up from the bottom of the shining dish. Yes, anyone who had trouble became his problem. He'd become a preacher to help folks, and even though Sarah got under his skin more than most—a lot more than most—she needed his help same as the others. It wasn't her fault he turned into a small schoolboy with his first crush each time she looked his way. All the promises he'd made God, had made himself, melted away when she turned her gaze in his direction.

He tugged at his collar, wondering if Redford knew what he was thinking. Well, what if he did? He stood. Tossing a coin on the table, he offered his hand to the sheriff, who argued, "Hey, I said my treat."

"Thank you for the company, sir. Let me treat this time to thank you for the use of your guest room." *And thank you so much for the hefty load of guilt you piled on my strudel. Thank you* very *much.* But he wouldn't mention that, not at the moment anyway.

"You come on around tonight. Molly will have your room all ready to go as usual. And if for any reason, like if anything comes up and you're delayed, I'll ask her to leave a sandwich on the sideboard, and you can help yourself to milk from the cellar. You know where everything is at. Same as always. Just make yourself at home."

"Thanks, Sheriff."

Strolling to Saul's side, TJ spied Banker Studdard. "Good day to you, sir."

Studdard walked right past him and placed a hand on Saul's mane, stroking the horse all the way down to his fetlock. "Fine animal you've got here."

"Yes, sir. The finest around these parts."

"He is that. How big would you say he stands?"

"He's a tad over eighteen hands. Why?"

"Ever thought of selling him?"

TJ laughed. "Well, sir, that would make my circuit a bit more difficult, don't you think? And without a wife, he's my one true companion." What on earth made him say that? Without a wife? He didn't want a wife. "No, sir. I'll not be selling him." He smiled and eased his leg over the saddle. "There's not enough money in the world to buy Saul."

With a tip of his hat, he pulled on the reins and left Studdard standing in a dusty heap.

TJ had seen it in his mind for the past month. He smiled at the familiar dirt road. Over and over he had remembered every detail riding into Gullywash and riding out. Where the scrub brush grew, where the slough grass still controlled an area. The small dotted areas of tree claims that were finally showing growth. But why would it fill his head, scene by scene? His life, perfect and orderly, kept him happy. Help folks, preach the Gospel and ride off on Saul. Best horse a man ever had… just as Studdard said. So why did a dirt road bring a smile to his lips? Because laughing brown eyes and blond curls lived along this road. And try as he might to rid his mind of her, he couldn't wait until he arrived at her door…to help Zach. Right.

The heat, more than he expected this time of year, lifted in waves from the ground. Too hot. He stopped Saul and drew a long cool drink of water from his canteen. He wiped his lips and looked ahead. He poured a bit into his hat and offered it to his horse. "How does that taste, boy? Nothing like a cold drink." The ground was a jumbling flurry of crickets, ants and caterpillars, all scurrying on their way. Almost as if they knew a secret that he should but didn't. Like in New York, where people hurried faster and faster to go nowhere in particular. He hopped back up on Saul. Not for him. Here he wasn't like the ants and grasshoppers; here he lived free and easy. No, once you had a family, the responsibility was overwhelming. Like Sarah and Zach. Their lives had turned upside down when Nathaniel had died, and she had to struggle each day to put food on the table and buy shoes for her boy. All the time wondering if a stranger would ride up and harm one of them.

But they weren't his problem. They weren't!

No sense stalling. He'd promised to help the boy as soon as he returned to town. No time like the present. He kicked gently into Saul's sides and they both trotted toward the Rycroft farm.

As he neared, he saw Zach playing in the front with the kitten close at hand. When the boy looked up and spotted TJ, he scrambled to his feet and for the front door, the kitten clawing at his side. "Mama. That man's here." He returned to the front. "Hello, Mis-ter—"

"O'Brien. How are you, young fella?"

"Jis waitin' for you to come back. Now we can saw and cut and paint."

"Whoa." TJ dropped over the side of the saddle. "Let's see that kitten of yours. She's getting mighty big, isn't she? We might have to build a bigger crate than I thought."

"Mama says Sassy loves mouses, er, mice. Loves mice. A lot."

"I'm sure she does. Did you collect the scrap wood like I told you?"

"Who's here?" Sarah Anne strolled onto the porch and placed her fists against her hips. "Well, it's the preacher. Why don't you come in and have some coffee and cookies before you get started on your project with Zach. I have wanted to talk with you. Did you see my wheat crop?"

"Fine-looking fields, ma'am."

She wiped her hands on an apron speckled with a

hard day's work. "I believe you agreed to call me Sarah or Sarah Anne. And you're...TJ, right?"

He loved the sound of her voice. The way it lifted at the end of words in a question whether she was asking one or not. A soft, gentle voice. Always gentle with the boy. "Yes, Sarah Anne. Call me TJ." He looked in Zach's direction. "And you, young fella, you go collect the wood. Bring it to the porch and we'll build us a crate, a new house, for Sassy."

"All right." The boy rushed from the porch on little legs in the direction of the barn, but he kept turning around, looking over his shoulder, no doubt to make sure TJ wasn't going to ride away and forget the promise.

"What did you want to discuss?"

Sarah poured the coffee, hot and strong, and placed a plate of warm oatmeal cookies with raisins next to his cup. "Since you're the preacher, I thought...well, I figured I'd tell you I planned to go to church meetings again."

"That's wonderful. What changed your mind, if it's not too personal?"

"Seems the good Lord has decided to bless me for a change. It feels like the right thing to do. You know. I owe Him or something like that." She smiled and felt the happiness crease from her lips to her eyes.

"Sarah Anne," he said, reaching for her hand, but in spite of the smile, she pulled back. "That's not why we love God. We don't wait for Him to do things for us. He's a God we love during bad times as well as good. We pray and hope and love Him, but we do it knowing that He might not answer the way we want."

"But He did, TJ. He's given me a wonderful wheat crop. It's going to be the answer, the right answer, to all my problems. I just know it. And I feel obligated, you see? So I figured it's time to teach Zach and start back myself."

Sarah realized he didn't understand because his life was happy. He didn't have responsibility, not a care in the world. How could he understand? He rode into town, preached a couple of sermons, patted a few widows' hands and rode out again. He hadn't ever needed to trust his God in troubled times.

She twisted a cloth napkin in her fingers. She wasn't being fair. His gaze dropped to her hands and she hid them beneath the table. His eyes began a brilliant steely search of her face. Sunlight through the window reflected on his thick black head of hair. One wave drooped over his forehead and she started to reach out and smooth it back but quickly snatched her hand away. She had no right.

"Sarah?"

"Nothing, I just… Well, I'm happy and I wanted to share it, that's all." She pushed the plate of cookies closer. "I thought you'd be happy."

"I am happy if you are. As long as you understand loving God isn't a trade-off for what He does for us." He finished a cookie in silence and smiled. "Mighty good cookies, if you don't mind my saying so."

She realized her expression had grown wary, but his statement unnerved her. "I don't mind. They're Zach's favorite. And the kitten has been known to eat a few crumbs, as well."

He grinned at her description of Zach and the kitten, both with milk lips and cookie crumbs on their faces.

Did the family stories endear them to him or make him want to run for cover? Sarah couldn't tell.

And she wasn't one to beg—not for anyone's attention.

Chapter 6

Zach placed the kitten in her new house and pulled her out. Put her in, pulled her out, until at last he was scratched for the effort. Sarah stopped staring out the window and called them in for supper to distract Zach. TJ lifted the boy on his shoulders and dashed for the house. "Let's wash those scratches, young man."

A couple sniffles preceded his "Okay."

"Looks like a gully washer overhead."

As they sprinted through the door, Zach laughed and pointed out the door at the dark clouds. "A gully washer in Gullywash, Mama." Then he stood on the chair in the kitchen and washed his hands as well as the scratches in the basin. "Yummy. Bacon gravy and biscuits. My favorite."

Sarah smiled. All food was his favorite. "Do you like gravy and biscuits, TJ?"

"I do. To be honest, I like almost any food that I don't have to cook. But are you sure? You didn't plan on me for supper."

With a tap of her toe to end any arguments, she said, "You helped Zach make a home for the kitty and you talked with me. I needed that. Thank you. It's hard not having an adult to speak with sometimes." She leaned close and with a whisper said, "I catch myself talking baby talk every now and then. Believe me, I like talking with a grown-up."

"I didn't think of that. I'm sorry."

She put her palms up. "Oh, don't be. When I start feeling like I have to be around folks other than a wee one and a kitty, I go to town and visit with Molly Redford. She's like a favorite aunt to Zach, and we both have a wonderful visit. You have no idea what I've learned from her. Almost like having another ma around. Then I don't miss mine so much."

TJ wiped the soap and water from his hands and neared the table. "I'm not sure how much help I was, but glad for the little bit that I did. I am known to be a good listener."

"That you are."

After prayers, he bit into the first biscuit, and she was delighted by his sigh. "Now, this is real food. Not like tack and too-strong coffee on the road."

"I'm glad you like it. We can have a couple smeared with apple butter after supper if you're still hungry."

Lightning crashed overhead. "Looks like I'm going to get a good soak before I make it back into town."

"If needs be, you can always bed down in the barn. I'll give you a blanket." No harm in letting him stay in the barn to protect himself.

"What would folks say?" He laughed a deep, husky laugh that brought a grin to her lips.

"Oh, dear. If my friends in this town don't have anything better to do than get worked up over stories about a preacher man and an old widow woman, then I don't know what."

"You're hardly an old widow woman."

Maybe not, but that was what lots of folks thought of her. And he wasn't exactly a common-looking preacher man. Did he think of her as more than an old widow? Did he think of her at all once he left Gullywash? She pressed her fingers to her hair, tucking stray curls behind her ear. She must look a mess. After all, she hadn't expected him back in town this soon.

By the time the cookies reappeared, Zach's eyes drooped when he cried, "Whus a wida woman, Mama?"

"Oh, dear. Look at that. Someone's very sleepy."

He stretched his arms out toward her. "Uh-huh."

"Excuse me, TJ. Seems I have a small one to put to bed." Zach must have been tired: he didn't even argue about being called a small one. And he didn't mention kitty.

"I should be on my way, as well."

"Are you going to ride back to town in this?"

"I could wait it out. If you don't mind."

"Pour yourself another cup of coffee. I'll be out in a minute. And maybe another cookie?" *He's been so kind to Zach. I owe him this at least.*

Who was she kidding? She enjoyed his company. He was handsome, caring, kind to Zach. He meant more than adult conversation; he had begun to mean a good friend. And if she were to be totally honest with herself, maybe even more than a friend.

A familiar thumping galloped in her chest. She'd promised herself never again, but here he was, doing all sorts of strange things to her heart.

"Would you like me to carry him for you?"

And kind to her, as well. "No, have your coffee in peace and quiet. And don't forget there are more cookies in the kitchen. I made plenty."

Besides, I need time away from your smiling face.

TJ finished his coffee and cleared the rectangular oak table that held a place of honor in the spacious front room. By the time Sarah had returned, the dishes had all been washed and dried and were waiting for her to put away. Cleaning their mess was the least TJ could do for the fine meal.

"Now, since when does a man do dishes?" Sarah smiled, and the smile did more than make him grin in return; it rippled through his stomach with a quiver, and he didn't exactly like the feeling. Too much. Was that what it meant to be a husband? Sharing responsibilities that he would do anyway as a courtesy and then having a woman smile and touch his heart?

"On the road, I do my own all the time." He wanted to say, "I'm alone and do for myself or it doesn't happen," but he didn't want sympathy. "Listen, Sarah—"

Thunder rolled overhead and lightning flashed long and hard. They both spun for the window when they saw a strike in the front yard. Sarah cried, "That one came too close."

They moved to the window, pulled the bleached muslin curtains back and stared out. TJ pointed toward the sky. "And there's more to come." Another flash followed immediately by thunder let them know just how close it was. "I will stay on if you are sure it won't compromise you in any way, Sarah."

She waved a hand. "I'm not one to listen to gossip, and I doubt my friends are, either. Once this lets up, you can go out in the barn and be warm and snug with a blanket. You can take the extra pillow from Zach's bed if you like."

"That won't be necessary. I have my own blanket and use my saddle if I need it."

Then TJ heard a cry at the door. "Hey, sounds like the kitty. May I let her in?"

"Oh, poor Sassy. I didn't think about her still outside. Of course you should let her in. She'll be soaked, even though she does have that fine house now." Her eyes lit up in an expression of playful gratitude.

He bowed. "A mansion, to be sure. And that little man of yours was doing a wonderful job of hauling the wood." He moved toward the front.

As he opened the door, the kitten ran inside, and TJ froze. A loud stuttering rattle began, along with the appearance of round hail the size of cherries, which pummeled the porch. Sarah Anne ran to the door. "No! *No!* It can't hail! My wheat!"

He grabbed her hands and pulled her away from the door before she could run out into the storm. "Sarah. Stop. You can't go out there." If this continued, there would be no reason to check on the wheat. *Lord, please, make it stop.* The entire crop would be ruined if the hail continued.

"But I have to save the crop! Please, help me!"

"You can't. There's nothing to be done, Sarah. The hail either stops or it doesn't. Let's wait it out."

Her eyes filled immediately with tears and he drew

her to his chest. She burrowed into the front of his blue chambray shirt and pressed against him. Warm tears flooded the front of him. He patted her hair and whispered in her ear, "This, too, shall pass. It's all right, Sarah. Cry if you like. I'm here."

Her fingers clutched into his shirt like claws as nature beat her wheat into the ground. "It won't pass. Hail will ruin the crop!"

"I understand, Sarah. Let's wait and see." He crushed her against him as if the closeness might take away her pain, her fear of the unknown. "Remember this—God's still in control." But TJ knew the wheat had been ruined by now. It didn't take that much pounding to destroy healthy stalks of wheat. Wheat that was days away from being harvested. Blood rushed in his ears. His own anger at the futility causing him to question his words.

She pulled away and looked into his eyes. "Sarah?" He lowered his head, waiting for her to invite him closer, and she did. His lips hovered over hers when another loud crash interrupted them.

She pressed palms against his chest and pushed—hard, her anger palpable in the room. "See there? That's what your God has for me. A ruined crop. It's fairly clear He's not going to do anything to help me. What have I done to make God hate me so?" She slumped to the floor. Cheeks that had previously blazed hot with rage were now pale and lifeless. She looked up, defeated. "Why, TJ? What makes Him want to hurt me like this? No matter what I do, what I try, God takes it away from me or destroys it. I thought He and I had come to an agreement."

TJ slid to the floor next to her. Moisture seeped

under the front door and soaked his pant leg. "C'mere."
He lopped his arm around her shoulder. "Sarah, God
doesn't work like that."

Her gaze bit into his, each word filled with mounting
frustration. "I don't want to talk about God. *Ever* again.
Don't want to think about Him or talk about Him."

"What *do* you want to talk about, Sarah? Tell me.
I'm here. I'll listen."

The question opened the floodgates as if her heart
wept through her eyes. "TJ, I have to bring that crop in
somehow. I have to. Without it I lose the entire farm.
Don't you understand? This is my last hope."

Thunder, like a slap in her already-downcast face,
roared around them, and more hail thudded against the
roof, the porch and...the wheat.

She straightened, smoothed her skirt over her legs,
drawing his gaze to her beautiful ankles. He looked
away. Not now, not now when her livelihood was drain-
ing away. Finding himself staring like a lovesick fool
set off warning bells in his head. *Offer kind words and
leave.* He couldn't. She needed this crop and he was here
to help guide her through a troubled time. The preacher
and the widow. That and nothing more.

He had to ask.

"Sarah, I understand this is none of my business,
but what will you do if you can't even up on the note
for the farm?"

"Don't worry about us." Her lip quivered again,
but she quickly set it to right by clamping tight with
her teeth. No sense airing all her dirty laundry with
this man.

"Sarah, please. I hope we're more than only a preacher and the widow Rycroft. Aren't we friends?"

Her manners were sorely lacking at that moment, but how could he understand? She saw the look of compassion in his eyes. Her personal life was safe with this man. "We have family in Boston. My mother and her husband. She remarried after my father died and sold our farm."

"So you grew up on a farm, as well?"

"Yes, but after Pa died, we left it. They took us to live in the city. I... Well, I don't plan to move in with them unless absolutely necessary. And Nathaniel's parents died when he was a youngster. I suppose his grandmother would take us in, but now that I'm out here where the land is open and fresh, I don't have any plans to return. I have to find a way to save this farm. It's my only chance."

The front window lit up and Sarah bit into her lip again so hard she drew a metallic taste into her mouth. Her fingers sought the tender point. Blood.

The preacher tipped her face up and asked, "What else is available for a woman and a child? Could you teach school? That's a respectable living and it should provide enough income for you and Zach."

"Oh, my, no. Not that I couldn't, I suppose. I simply would not want to unless it was a last resort. I hear enough 'How comes' and 'Whats' from Zach all day long. I'm not sure I'd be ready to hear the same from fifteen or twenty other children every day. I've always been more of a hands-on worker. That's one reason Nathaniel and I decided to go west. He knew he had a willing manual laborer in me. Other than cooking and cleaning, I enjoy dipping my hands in the soil and watching things grow." She fumbled with her hands in her lap while TJ's arm burned against her back. She glanced up and found his face far too close. If either of them moved an inch, they would be kissing.

She shook her head. What had made her think such a thought? Her entire world was collapsing around her and she was dwelling on the preacher's lips.

Her heart thudded, betraying her resolve to never care again. While the wind screamed around her, no doubt destroying the very crop that allowed for independence from another man, she melted against TJ's strength. She had fought so long by herself, fighting not only the elements but men who predicted her failure. Men like Banker Studdard. She shuddered. Barely more than a month to make good.

Arms like bands of steel tightened, offering their own sense of security. Sarah licked her lips and closed her eyes. TJ's chin rested on her head. Enclosed in the safe, warm cocoon, she could almost believe everything would be all right. She could almost think God was out there somewhere, caring about what happened to her, but the sound of hail rattled that thought from her mind. God didn't care a bit about her or Zach or the farm. And warm arms as a temporary refuge didn't change that fact.

"I have to go see what happened." She started to push away, but TJ pushed back, his gaze trailing over her like a calm breeze.

"Wait until the lightning stops."

Wait, wait for what? The entire farm to wash away. *Gullywash* meant something entirely new to her now. "But—"

He tightened his grip. "I'll go with you when it

stops. We'll see the fields together, Sarah. Right now it wouldn't be safe for either of us to go out in the storm."

Another lightning strike convinced her he was right.

After the storm finally abated, the once-thick heads of grain lay limp in her hands. Sarah picked up another and another and another, sobbing the whole time, until TJ couldn't tell if it was rain or tears running over her cheeks. "All of it," she whispered.

"Looks that way, all right."

Sarah's gaze stuttered over the field, left and right, and she dropped the battered wheat, brushing grainy residue from her hands. "I've never seen such damage before. Not even in all the years Pa farmed. Nothing ever like this. TJ, my entire crop." Her gaze locked on to the worst of it, and she froze, staring, her eyes devoid of any more emotion.

TJ didn't think anything he said would make a difference. Her chance to save her farm had been pounded into the ground. Not a stalk of wheat stood. There had been hail the size of walnuts before the storm ended. TJ had held out little hope any of the wheat could be saved, and he had been right. Whole fields lay flat in row after row of mud.

At last Sarah moved enough to tug a hankie from her sleeve, then wiped her eyes and blew her nose. She stood tall and surveyed her land like a child with a lost puppy out there somewhere. Helpless, frightened, crushed by the loss but still searching as if it might reappear.

If only words would come to him, an opportunity to say something meaningful that might lift her up, give her hope. TJ tried to hold her hand, but she brushed him away and dashed from his side. Before she'd crossed two rows, her feet sloshed in the mucky field, the wheat unable to stop her feet from sinking, and he simply stayed put, unable to offer any words of condolence. The crop was ruined. Not a stalk remained. When the note came due at the end of September, she would lose it all. *Why, God? Hasn't she lost enough?*

He breathed in the horrid smell of wet earth and destruction, trying to discern one from the other. But it was a mishmash of mud, battered vegetation and, if it was possible, the stench of death. Maybe it only seemed that way, but TJ was certain he smelled death in the earth. Perhaps it was simply the hopeless end of what was supposed to have meant life to Sarah and Zach.

Before TJ could stop her, Sarah dropped to her knees, sank half a foot into the ground. "Why?" she cried over and over, the sound turning into a mournful chant, worse than what he'd heard at funerals. "God, why do You hate me so? What have I done to deserve Your wrath? Am I really such a bad person?"

Hurrying and slipping in the mud, TJ landed by her side. He dropped to the ground next to her and wrapped her in his arms. "Shh, Sarah. God didn't do this. Please. Don't blame Him. Sarah Anne, God loves you. Turn back to God." There, he'd said the words he had wanted to say since he first met her, but all the while he wondered the same thing. *You might not have caused this, Lord, but why did You allow it to happen?*

Trust. The only sound in his heart. *Trust. But, Lord, it's so hard to trust when all of this is happening. Trust.* One word to stand on, and he was pretty sure she wouldn't want to hear it.

Sarah ripped from his grasp, struggled to her feet and

picked up what was left of a stalk of wheat. "Turn back to God? He loves me?" Without hesitation she threw the stalk in his face. "I hate that your God has let this happen to me. Do you hear me! Leave me alone! Go away, Preacher! And take your God with you! Since you came along with your words of His love and caring, my life has been ripped from me. That's right. Zach and I have nothing left!"

TJ wiped the wheat off his face and reached for her hand. But her eyes sparked with hatred. His words would be a poor source of comfort. She was right; he hadn't been able to help them. "You'd better go on in. Zach's in the house alone."

Sarah's gaze strengthened and looked beyond him to a place he was no longer welcome. He turned and mucked his way to the barn, where Saul waited to go back to town.

Go away, Preacher! And take your God with you!
The words were no sooner off her lips than Sarah longed to take them back. She didn't mean it, didn't hate the preacher *or* God. Not really. But the hurt that clawed its way through her gut, her mind and even her heart was killing her one feeling at a time. How long before this hatred would find its way to how she treated Zach? She'd been a long time coming around from Nathaniel's death, hadn't given Zach the care he'd needed. If not for Molly… She shuddered. She couldn't allow that kind of melancholy to happen again.

Zach needed her common sense, her strength. He needed to know that somehow, somewhere, they would find hope again. And if she didn't present that face of certainty, he would feel it all the way to his gut. Even as young as he was, he would know and understand she had no hope.

She watched as TJ O'Brien trudged through the mud and finally reached the barn. How he must dislike her— hate her. No, hate lived only in her heart, but he must be terribly disappointed in the way she had acted. What a mess she'd made of her life recently. A huge mess that couldn't be undone. This field the biggest mess of all. No matter how far she looked, all she saw was muck and broken stalks of wheat. The earth had been so thirsty it had soaked in the rain until it could hold no more. Now mud covered everything.

She choked back another sob, her hankie now streaked with dust, tears and pieces of wheat. The only crop she could see from all this destruction was a field of rich soil once this land was plowed under.

Sarah fell forward, her face landing against the ground. Pushing up, face covered in mud, she understood her way wasn't working. She couldn't bargain with God for a better future. With nothing left in her control, she took her plea to Him, her heart hungry to hear what He really wanted of her. And yet she had to speak from deep within where all the questions burned at her. *Oh, Lord, why? I thought we had everything worked out. You bring in a good crop for me and I'd start believing again, in a good God, a God who cares. But You don't care. You didn't take care of my crop. Why should I keep my part of the bargain? Do You expect me to serve a God who causes a woman with no husband to lose everything? Why would I want to do that?*

She struggled to stand, but the weight of her grief drove her farther into the mud until she was lying fully against the ground, her face and hands covered in it.

Had anyone felt this low before? Been this discouraged? Breath caught in her throat. Christ had obviously felt discouragement and pain…nothing like this. Worse. Much worse. How could she feel sorry for herself when He had endured so much…for her. A widow. A farmer.

The realization, like a slug in the gut, brought her around. In all of her self-pity, never once had she thought of what He'd endured. All she had cared about was making a bargain with Him to better her life. Was that all He'd been to her?

Lord, I can't fight You any longer. I can't. If You take everything and everyone I love, I can't fight You. You mean more than that. Please show me what You want from me. I give in. You are bigger than all of my problems, all of them. And I don't really have the right to complain. You are the One who gave it all. Not me and my pitiful farm. You gave Your Son.

Sarah lay in the mud for what seemed to be an hour or more. The rain had stopped and a warmth curled through her. She reached out and touched small mounds of the chilling hail, but it wasn't cold. Warmth fell across her…as her grandmother's quilt had when she had been a child fighting a cold. Crawling under the quilt's warmth had begun the healing, cradled in its layers of comfort. Like a life-healing balm.

She *would* get better. With God's help she'd find a way to save her farm, and if she couldn't, then God would open another door for her and Zach. And whatever He wanted, she would try to accept.

Once the tears ended, she sat up, surveying the field. Her heart hitched against her chest, but the pain didn't return. She longed to talk with TJ again, but she couldn't. Not yet. The confused mess that she was at the moment would only make him question her even more. No, she had to let him go. If he came back on his own, then she would talk to him about this night. This night that even she didn't fully understand yet.

Chapter 7

He'd failed as a preacher. His heart breaking into thousands of tiny pieces, TJ rode in silence to the sheriff's house. He couldn't even bring comfort to the beautiful widow Rycroft. Beautiful.... Was that why? He had begun to think of her as a beautiful woman instead of a lost soul in need of Christ. He hadn't kept his distance. He had begun to fall in love, if truth be known, and that wasn't allowed. All of his noble promises came crashing in around him. He had begun to think far too much of himself and his ability to make a difference. *Forgive me, Lord. Forgive my pride and veering from what You want of my life.*

His life belonged to God. To the open road so he could preach and not have distractions. He had betrayed his own calling. To serve God. To think only of Him. Wasn't that the promise he'd made ten years ago in New York.

The memories flooded his brain. It was as if he were back in New York, in that crowded tenement.

TJ remembered watching as another child died. First the rash, then the cough and runny nose, sore throat and swollen neck. It seemed that the scarlet fever passed easily from one child to the other, as families lived close together. But hadn't the doctor told them it didn't spread that way? And yet TJ saw one child sick, then another sick, until three of the five small children living in the dank room they all shared had died. TJ was sixteen years old in 1871. The last baby had taken ill. Seeing the rash covering the infant's cheeks, TJ dropped to his knees as he bathed the wee boy. He already loved reading his uncle's Bible, and giving his life to God was a simple step but one that meant commitment to him even at such an age.

Father, I'm not here to bargain with You, and yet that is exactly what is in my heart. Please, Lord. Save these last two children of Mr. and Mrs. McEnnery. Father, they brought their young ones here to have a better life in America, and now they have lost three babes, and they're young themselves. But You know that; I'm not telling You a thing You don't know. I'm begging You to save the babies, Lord. I will give You my life in exchange. For the rest of my life, I will preach Your word, love the lost, give to those in need, and I will do it with a grateful, cheerful heart. I promise You this, Lord. Just let the babies live. And I will be Yours forever to go where You will and do what You will. Nothing will stop me from that task. I vow to You, Lord.

The babies had lived. And TJ had been raised by his uncle to be a man of honor, so he hadn't questioned for one second what he must do.

When his parents died, he was only six, and he had nowhere to go but New York to live with his uncle.

Uncle Michael took care of the poor, and his modest apartment in the middle of the city had become home to twelve people. Five slept in the small bedroom and the others slept on blankets anywhere they found space. His uncle could not say no to the poor who came begging at his door. One family of seven and one small family of three. And TJ and his uncle gave all their room to help. Had another come begging, he would no doubt have slept *under* the mattress if necessary.

TJ smiled, remembering his uncle's favorite joke. But today with Sarah had been no joke. All of his lofty promises had been forgotten for a pretty face, and he had left her worse off than he had found her and the boy. If she'd had doubts about God before, they had grown into monsters, filling her heart and engulfing her with fear. And it was all TJ's fault.

Sarah gazed around her cozy room. A room Nathaniel had built with care. He'd made the rope bed in one day, anxious for them to have a place of their own. While he cut and pegged and stretched the heavy rope, Sarah had aired and restuffed the feather tick they'd been given as a wedding gift. At last they'd fallen into bed too tired to even kiss one another good-night. But they had snuggled into the soft comfort of the feather tick in the knowledge of love and caring.

The memory brought a smile as she crawled into bed exhausted, worry not far from the wonderful memories. She would make every attempt to understand that all of her problems were in God's hands, but still the worries churned through her mind. Maybe her shortcomings needed more than one day to change. She smiled. The only difference now was that somehow things would work out, and if that meant she had to return to Boston to live with her mother or with Nathaniel's grandmother, then so be it. Leaving Gullywash would break her heart but never again her spirit. This evening she had come too far to ever go back. God had truly brought her to her knees with nowhere to look but up, and from now on she wanted only to go forward. With His help, she vowed to do just that.

TJ O'Brien. He had looked at her with so much hurt in his eyes. Instead of the gentle smile she was used to seeing, there had almost been a look of anger. Well, why not? She'd behaved horribly toward him. Toward God. From the minute he'd stepped foot on their farm asking for a cool drink of water, her lack of hospitality had shown. So what did she have the right to expect from him?

She turned to her side and stared at the wall. No time to think about the preacher. Not now. Plans had to be made for the farm. She would see Banker Studdard in the morning. Perhaps he would consider… She didn't know what. Part of her field as payment? Surely he wouldn't put her out. Who else would buy this property—in this condition?

Her lofty ideas fell at last under heavy eyelids, and she succumbed to sleep.

When she awakened in the morning, Sarah wasted no time over breakfast. The sourdough hotcakes with molasses and milk filled their bellies in a hurry. "Get a move on, Zach. We have to get cleaned up for town." After seeing the banker, she intended to find the preacher and apologize for her rude behavior last night. Maybe he'd listen, maybe not, but she had to try.

* * *

Sheriff Redford lounged against the hitching post, early-morning sun casting his shadow behind him. The hot sun was already causing Sarah to sweat under her bonnet. But her mind wasn't on shadows or sweat; it was on the preacher.

"That's right, Sarah. He left first thing after breakfast."

She couldn't believe her ears. "Gone? Where did he go? He's supposed to be in Gullywash for church on Sunday. Who will preach in his place?"

"Not this Sunday, Sarah. He got word a friend passed on. A Mr. Merriweather or Merriton, something or other."

"Merriman," she offered. "Mr. Merriman. Yes, he said the man was very ill. They didn't really expect him to live." How sad for the family even if the man was getting up in age.

The sheriff offered a sad smile, obviously realizing how talk of a funeral brought up bad memories for Sarah. "So he hightailed out of town this morning. Said he'd be back in a month. We won't have services at the saloon this Sunday." He wiped his brow, the heat after the storm steamy and thick. "Anything I can do to help you, ma'am?"

Her heart pounding, Sarah turned away. "No, thank you, Sheriff Redford. I appreciate you telling me." She spun back around. "Wait. Is Molly home today?"

"Last I saw her. Why? She was baking my favorite cookies. I told her not to, the heat being so oppressive and all, but she does love to please. A good woman, my Molly." He patted his stomach and grinned.

Sarah returned the smile. "I thought she might see

to Zach. I need to speak with Banker Studdard and I'd rather he not be with me." *I'd rather not be there myself. Facing Studdard, having to beg for my farm. No, I don't want Zach with me.*

The sheriff reached down and patted Zach on the head. "Why, you just know she'd love to see the boy. You run on along and I'll take him to the house." He winked at Zach, who waited beside Sarah. "We might stop for a horehound stick or a gingerbread man if it's all right."

Sarah waited for Zach's reply. "Say yes, Mama?" His hands pressed between his knees, he jumped from foot to foot, the excitement too much for him.

"Yes, Mama," Sarah repeated. She laughed and ruffled his stuck-up hair until it plastered flat—for a second. Then she eyed the big lawman. "I'm not sure who the bigger child is here, Sheriff."

Zach's hand was dwarfed in Redford's as he skipped across the muddy street trying to keep up with the big steps of the sheriff. Her son shot a gaze over his shoulder, then giggled and waved at Sarah. What a beautiful boy she had.

Twenty feet away the bank loomed in front of her like a giant, the door a mouth waiting to devour her and her farm. But she had no choice. The crop was gone, and the only option she had at this point was to beg Studdard to give her more time.

Sarah entered the bank and took a seat in a heavy wooden chair near the door. She didn't tell anyone she was there, but soon Myra Brekenridge called her over. "You want to see Mr. Studdard?"

"Yes, I guess so."

Myra offered a sympathetic smile. "You aren't the

first one this morning." The sorrowful expression told Sarah everything the woman was afraid to put into words.

Sarah clutched her clean handkerchief to her chest. All the farmers in the area must have lost their crops. Families she knew. Families she and Nathaniel had called friends. What could the banker do to fix their problems? Might he turn everyone out?

"Mrs. Rycroft," the banker said, his smile as oily as a fried chicken, "won't you follow me?" He offered his well-manicured hand in such a condescending way her stomach churned. This was a useless effort, but she had to try.

She stood and took his hand in spite of it making her feel dirty. "I had hoped we could talk about—"

"First we'll ask Mrs. Brekenridge for a cup of tea. All right? Then we'll both feel better."

She wouldn't. A cup of tea couldn't raise her crop from the ground. "Thank you, but I'd rather talk to you about last night's storm."

He patted her hand as her father used to when she was a child, but this hand didn't offer hope—it ensnared her like a rabbit with a gun barrel aimed at its face. "There, there. A great many farmers have been affected by the terrible storm." As he lifted his arm, a nasty odor emanated from him. She didn't expect that, only with the heat… Well, why should she be surprised?

"So you've already considered options for a great many of us. I'm relieved." But she didn't feel at all relieved. His expression didn't hint at relief.

"*However,* I am afraid that most of them have other sources of income. Take Barnabus Felton. He has two fields of corn that should help him get by. The corn stood up to the hail. You chose to put in only wheat, Mrs. Rycroft. And the wheat is what was destroyed, don't you know." He held up a hand and inspected the back as though one might inspect a piece of fine jewelry. "You see, Mrs. Rycroft, the *men* put in different crops with the knowledge that they could have trouble in planting only one. They have the ability to farm sensibly. Like men."

Like men. He certainly didn't mince words.

"They all put in more than wheat?"

"Not all. A few were foolish like you. They shouldn't have been, but they'll soon see the folly of their ways." Like a woman, she supposed. "And some weren't hit so hard. Only lost a portion of their crop."

How could she ask for more time? She had to. "I thought if you could extend the note a bit longer, maybe I could get a winter wheat in for next spring. I doubt lightning is going to strike two seasons in a row."

He patted her hand again, and she wanted to pull away, but if it made him feel fatherly, then so be it. "Now, now. I doubt that field could be readied in time. My son has started lessons again with Franklin Sauer, and I simply can't allow him to miss in order to help you this fall." His head shook side to side, and all the while he tsked and harrumphed, apparently to end the conversation. "As much as I ache to be of assistance to you, I simply cannot allow you to have more time with the note."

Of course he could allow it. He'd allowed it last spring when his son wanted money to buy a horse. Between money and the piglet, which he'd raised and would sell, that time away from his lessons hadn't seemed to have bothered Studdard any. And if he thought she was going to back down, he had another think coming.

"Perhaps with a couple extra months, I might be able to come up with another way to pay off the note."

"Mrs. Rycroft, you were already extended six months so you could put in a crop. I didn't agree with your trying. I thought you should sell, but you wanted a chance to prove yourself. I'm afraid the best thing you can do is find a buyer for the farm, and I have told you I will buy it from you for a small profit, enough that you and the boy can return to Boston. Shall we say fifty dollars over the note? That and what you sell of your personal items should give you a tidy nest egg to start once you return east. Where you belong."

She saw his oily smile again, like a snake swallowing a gopher whole. He acted as though she were the gopher! Well, he had no idea who he was dealing with. Sarah Anne Rycroft, wife of Nathaniel Zachary Rycroft, wasn't so easily swayed. But she didn't need to let him read all of her thoughts right away.

"Perhaps we'll return." Boston. Not exactly what she'd planned. She'd hated the thought of the city once she had viewed the open prairie, milked a cow, rode a horse around the property. She would miss all of that, but what choice did she have? Well, no matter what, not Boston.

"Well, child? What do you think?"

I think you're plainly anxious to have my property. But she didn't say that to his face. A niggling feeling slithered through her insides like a worm tunneling through the ground. He wanted her property so much he was offering to buy and give her a profit? Why hadn't she seen this before? Banker Studdard had set out to see her fail. He had wanted her to plant. He'd hoped to get more for his money when she couldn't bring the crop in. So now he offered a piddling profit to encourage her to give up. His plan had worked to his advantage. No matter what had happened, he would be left with the property in better condition than before she had plowed.

"It's not right a lady like you should be trapped in this wilderness. It's a hard enough life when a woman has a husband to care for her, all the harder when she doesn't. This is no place for a lady, Mrs. Rycroft. If you'd be honest with yourself, you'd admit that. You deserve to return to the city, where you'll enjoy parties and conveniences. Pretty dresses and buggy rides. Special dinners and teas."

"I didn't grow up in the city, Mr. Studdard. I grew up on a farm, and my father believed in young ladies helping outside. With *all* aspects of the farm. He said the sun and fresh air was good for both girls and boys. I loved being on a farm. I still do."

"Foolish stuff and nonsense. Your parents catered far too much to your whims instead of to your proper upbringing."

Sarah felt her hackles rise. "I beg your pardon. Do not impugn my parents, Mr. Studdard. I'll thank you to leave them out of this conversation. My father proved himself a wonderful parent time and again."

He sniffed into his handkerchief and held up his hand to stop her. "Very well, but your hard work is all the more reason to take time for yourself now. Why, you'll turn into a city girl in no time at all, and the opportunities for the boy will be unlimited. If you'll sell the farm to me this week, I'll make all of your preparations for you and your little boy to go back east. And I know I shouldn't. Really shouldn't." He shook his head. "But I'm willing to go sixty dollars over your note. Enough for a good start. Plus—" he held up his hand "—two tickets home. On my sawbuck. After all, as a member of the newly formed church, I feel it's my duty to help a widow and her boy. That's in scripture, you know."

Blood thudded in her ears to think of him daring to talk scriptures to her. "Yes, I am well aware."

"Well, then." He slapped his hands together. But his words, coarse and senseless, sent shivers all through her body. She didn't believe the concern he tried to show her. And she wasn't exactly sure why. "Let me draw up the papers today. How would that be?" He was all smiles now.

Home. Her mother and that man she'd married. The shivers Sarah had just felt from Mr. Studdard's fingers were nothing compared to the awful feeling she got whenever she was around her mother's husband. No, she would not go back to Boston, nor would she live with Nathaniel's grandmother, though she was a delightful lady. This was her home. Hers and Nathaniel's. No, hers and Zach's. And her farm was where she intended to raise her boy, not in some school back east.

"Mr. Studdard, I'm afraid I'll take my chances."

In an instant, his face turned pricklier than a porcupine's back. "You'll what!" His cheeks flamed and his eyes bulged angrily, all fatherly pretense gone. Here was the true Banker Studdard.

"I intend to find another way to pay the note."

"There is no other way, young woman! Now, my offer is only good until tomorrow morning. You have until eleven o'clock to come to your senses. Not a minute more."

"Then—" she gazed at the huge clock on the banker's bookshelf "—I have twenty-five hours to discover a way to save my farm." She rose from the chair, doing her best to keep from crying. Because in all honesty, she didn't have a clue how to manage the impossible task. But she wouldn't give him the satisfaction of knowing that. Not today anyway. "Good day, Mr. Studdard."

He huffed a response she didn't hear well and wasn't about to ask him to repeat. No doubt words a lady shouldn't be subjected to. She kept walking straight toward the door, past Mrs. Brekenridge's startled face. Twenty-five hours. Oh, my, what *had* she promised?

Chapter 8

Eighty-year-old Mrs. Henry Merriman sniffled and pressed her nose into her hankie. Over the course of an hour, TJ patted her hand, offered to get her more tea and made what he thought were appropriate responses. The woman had aged before his eyes, but still she tried to smile and make the best of her circumstance.

"Such a good man," Mrs. Merriman repeated for at least the tenth time. "You didn't know him well, did you Mr. O'Brien?"

He eased back in the chair. "Why, Hank and I were fine friends, Mrs. Merriman. You know that. Who took him hunting the week before he took ill? We didn't catch anything, but we tried. Oh, how we tried. And we had a mighty fine time of it."

Mrs. Merriman suddenly smiled, creases crisscrossing her face. "Didn't you, though? Henry told me how he took aim and fell over. Couldn't stop laughing about that." She frowned. "I wonder now if that fall wasn't the first sign of apoplexy that took him ill. But he did have a grand time. And instead of wild rabbit on a fire, you ate butter-and-honey sandwiches I'd packed. My, but you two did enjoy each other's company. Who would have guessed, a couple preachers out hunting?"

TJ's brow lifted. "A couple preachers?"

"Lands, yes. Henry didn't tell you? He preached the Gospel until you came along. As he added years, he grew tired, and you were a breath of fresh air. Fresh words, too, if truth be told. Henry had lost his ability to put fresh thoughts to his sermons long ago, and we both rejoiced when you found us. I'm surprised Henry didn't tell you."

"He didn't say a word. I wasn't privy to his lack of ability."

She returned the favor and patted his hand. "Maybe he saw fit to let you step in easily, not feel as if there were any competition. He admired you, my boy. And the folks hereabout were plumb ready to hear some fresh preaching. Poor Henry. He'd taken to repeating not only words but sermons week after week. I didn't have the heart to tell him how forgetful he was becoming."

"He was a good man." TJ smiled, happy with the direction their conversation had taken. "Would you like a warm-up for your tea?"

"I'll be fetching it for you, boy." Spark returning, Mrs. Merriman waddled to the stove, favoring her right hip. "I'm not about to stop being hospitable because of a few aches and pains. I guess I can still wait on you." She hefted the pot with shaky hands and brought him hot water to add to his cup as well as hers.

She, too, was slipping. Unable to perform her daily chores. He wouldn't bring it to her attention, though. "Just what I needed. A warm-up. I'm obliged." He spooned more honey into his cup and blew on the watered-down tea.

Once she returned to her seat, he leaned forward to face Mrs. Merriman directly. "May I ask you a rather personal question?"

She poured tea into her saucer and watched it as if it might slide right over the side. "If you like. I have very few secrets." Dimples peppered her wrinkled face and comfort oozed through him. She would stay in their home until she couldn't move without help.

Now her grin reminded him of a young girl's. She liked to talk about her life with Henry. That was obvious. "Mrs. Merriman, did Henry ever have trouble separating himself from his life with God?"

"I'm not sure what you mean." She sipped tea from the saucer with a slurp and then giggled like a small girl. "Sorry. I don't have the strength I once did. Tipsy, like the men in the saloon. Gracious, I wish I could move about like the young girl I was when I met Henry."

"I mean, did your family stand in the way of his preaching from time to time? Was he able to balance his family and his time spent preaching? I've always thought a man couldn't do justice to both."

Her change in demeanor startled him. Lost was the smile; here was the look of a preacher's wife who had serious wisdom to impart, and he intended to listen. "Young man, marriage is the embodiment of God. Don't you believe that?"

"Certainly. I know Jesus takes the Church as his bride."

"No, it's even simpler than that. God is the father of the family. Rather stern at times but always loving no matter what. Then His Son, Jesus, is like the mother of the family. She goes to the father on behalf of the children the same way Christ is the one who takes the responsibility for his children, then takes their sins on Himself before going to the Father. He's all-loving and caring and nurturing. I do believe that is why Jesus calls the little children to him, just like a mother pulls her children to her breast. He feeds us, nurtures us, don't you know, and goes to our Father on our behalf. The same way mothers do to help their little ones avoid a trip to the woodshed."

He rubbed his chin with his hand. "I didn't think of it that way. But when you say it like that—"

Mrs. Merriman leaned toward him and planted a light kiss on his cheek. "Dear boy, there are many verses in scripture that point to the family as the most important creation the good Lord ever made. A loving father, a protecting father, and children, the precious hope of the future."

But what about the promise? He had made a promise to God.

"What about when he traveled around? Didn't your sons feel left out?"

"That's where a good woman comes in. A preacher's wife must be understanding. A little extra goes a long way, my boy. Why, I used to dig worms for the boys. I didn't have the ability to take Henry's place, but I did my best. And I was rewarded by respect from Henry and the joy of my boys."

"You did what? Worms?" He was sure his look

betrayed his disbelief. Dear old Mrs. Merriman dug worms?

"Oh, lands, yes. I taught our boys how to go out after a rain and find the biggest, fattest worms you ever saw. For a while there, they had a worm farm. Not sure why they wanted a worm farm, but they had the finest one in these parts." That memory made her giggle again. "Probably the only one in these parts, if truth be told. Lands, the worm farm. Why, I haven't thought of that in years."

He shook his head and chuckled. "You amaze me."

She waved her frail hand like a small flag. "Did my job. I was his better half for sure and for certain. And he knew that he could count on me for whatever had to be done. I was his eyes and ears when he was away. I didn't ever tell my boys to wait for a dusting of their pants until their daddy got home. I took the oldest to the woodshed a time or two myself, but not often. They were good boys. Yes, I took care of the sick and dying, too, like you are caring for me today." She nodded knowingly, as if a recollection was taking her to another time...another place. "And Henry, the dear man, always paid in full. He loved me, Preacher. Loved me like no man had ever loved a woman before." Her cheeks pinked and he looked away. "Oh, I've said too much. Embarrassed you, boy. I'm sorry."

Women were stronger creatures than he had ever believed. Without a mother's influence in his life, he hadn't been afforded the luxury of that understanding. Was Sarah like Mrs. Merriman?

"No, it's all right. I'm proud you felt you could confide in me."

If he asked to see Mrs. Rycroft to dinner one evening, would she agree? No. He raked his hand through his hair, his best thinking gesture. He'd made a promise that he had to keep. Good woman or not, he had caused Mrs. Rycroft's problems because he hadn't kept his place. He had to remember what his calling was and be true to it. Falling for a beautiful widow didn't fit into his plan.

"Thank you, Mrs. Merriman. I should have been consoling you, and you, as usual, have helped me. You are a dear friend and your husband will be sorely missed."

"Why don't you finish your cookies and tea, dear? My daughter-in-law will be here soon. I'll be fine. You've been a kind young man. May I tell you something?"

"Of course. What is it?"

"You find a woman to stand by you the way I stood by my Henry all these years. Be sure she has strength, so important, and make sure she's a believer and good with children. She'll keep your feet warm in the winter, too."

This time his face flushed.

"Oh, pshaw. Don't be a fainting flower. We're grown folk. A good woman will warm your bed, love you when you aren't all that lovable and she'll see to your needs in good times and bad. Whether you're a strapping young man or an old fellow, like Henry. That's true happiness. As close to heaven on earth as you'll find." She grinned a sassy smile. "You have a houseful of babies like we did, and you'll see the hand of God on all you do. Blessings, my boy."

TJ rose, the blessing etched onto his heart, but he had a calling. No room for love or any other nonsense, in spite of how it warmed his heart to hear of her love of Henry.

Sarah counted the coins and added them to the rest of the money. She had been able to save twenty-two dollars in the past six months. If only she could sell four of the young pigs, two of the cows, two calves, maybe eighteen, even twenty of the chickens and the team of horses. A good team that Nathaniel had trained well. She should be able to raise $180 or thereabouts. Maybe even more with the right buyer. That would give her just over the $200 she needed to pay off the note. Maybe then she'd have enough to hire someone so the field could be plowed under and she could plant a winter crop. She couldn't part with Lightfoot, her other horse. She needed her to pull the wagon should they have to leave and go back home. Couldn't sell the rifle, as she had to be able to keep Zach safe. Besides, Nathaniel had caressed that rifle with oil every night. He'd loved it as he loved a woman: with everything he had and with gentle hands.

All right, Lord. I'm not going to start crying all over again. This is in Your hands. I've done all I can to put things to right. Now, well, now it's up to You.

As soon as Zach was dressed, she would load him into the wagon along with the squawking chickens, and they would start going farm to farm in order to sell off her surplus animals. She'd make bargains so the farmers couldn't resist. By tomorrow she hoped to have the $200 she needed.

* * *

Sarah fought tears. The comfortable farmhouse had been her last hope. "But, Mr. Felton, I know your wife raises eggs to sell. These are strong laying hens. You won't find them any less expensive. Please. I know you lost your wheat, too, but you still have corn. I have only my animals to try and save my farm."

Barnabus Felton wrung his hands in front of him. "Real sorry, ma'am, but I can't afford to spend any money right now. I'm sure you understand."

"But you have—"

"Mama, don't cry." Zach's face mirrored her own. Sad, trembling lips, downcast eyes. Did she really look that bad? Here she stood in front of her neighbor begging for their livelihood.

She nodded toward Mr. Felton. "I thank you for hearing me out, Mr. Felton."

"Real sorry, ma'am. I am that." His fingers plucked his overalls like guitar strings, nervously explaining more than his words. She knew his wife had been asking about more good hens. Why, then, would he balk at purchasing hers? Everyone in town knew from Mrs. Haley what fine layers they were.

All day long, driving the wagon in the hot sun from farm to farm, Sarah met with the same answers. "Very sorry, ma'am. I respected your husband, but I just can't come up with cash money for you." One farmer after another until she and Zach arrived at Mr. Swenson's farm.

"What you say you have beside t'em chickens?"

She felt her face twist into a knot. "Two cows and two calves—one a bull calf—four young pigs and a team of horses, trained to harness. Good sturdy horses. Nathaniel broke them before he passed on. I wouldn't

sell them, only...I really need the money, Mr. Swenson."
Frightened just standing next to the big Swede who had
arrived only months ago, Sarah worked the edge of her
lip, nipping skin already tender from the nervous irritating habit. "All of the animals have been well cared
for. I can assure you."

His frown, heavy and deep, stared her down. "I am
new to your town, but I am not fool, Mrs. Rycroft. I
hear t'ings."

"You hear things? What things? I'm asking a very
fair price, Mr. Swenson. And this is prime stock. Nathaniel bought and raised only the best animals."

"Fair? You asked fair price? For t'em sick animals?"

She stumbled back, her hand over her heart. "Sick
animals? My animals are all healthy and strong. Right
down to the last chicken's egg. How dare you accuse
me—"

"You leave my land. Now! Fair? You leave, Mrs. Rycroft. Lady or not lady, you must go."

"Who said I have sick animals, Mr. Swenson? Who?"

His face twisted into an angry portrait, and his lips
clamped tight. Someone was undermining her sale of
the livestock. But who would do such a thing?

Sarah reached for his arm and tugged at his shirt. "I
have a right to know who would spread lies like that. I
know you're new here, Mr. Swenson, but I'm an honest person."

"Don't you yell at my mama," Zach cried. "Our pig-
gies and chickens aren't sick!"

"Shh, Zach, please." Sarah pushed her son behind
her. "Who, Mr. Swenson?" But Zach pressed around
her side, landing in front of her, every bit the minia-

ture of her husband, arms crossed in front of him and brow furrowed.

Swenson's fingers curled around the rope in his hand. "Mr. Studdard," he mumbled. "He tell me you try to sell sick animals. I don't talk too good, but I not fool, ma'am. You leave my farm. Take t'em sick animals. And go." He pointed across his property and Sarah leaped into the wagon, tears that had been pouring over her cheeks now dried from the heat of her skin. Banker Studdard!

"Zachary, into the wagon." She tugged at his arm as his little legs scrambled onto the front seat...where his father had always sat. "You all right, son?"

He sat ramrod straight, eyes locked on to the road, every bit the boy trying to be her protector. "I'm fine, Mama. Let's go."

Neither of them looked back, the realization swirling in Sarah's gut that Studdard would stop at nothing to get his hands on her property, including lying.

Her voice, if not her gaze, fell on Swenson as she drove away. "I don't lie, Mr. Swenson, and if you think that of your new neighbors, you won't feel a particularly warm welcome in Gullywash."

Chapter 9

TJ finished the service in Tideville and paid his respects to all the folks in town. The Werners had him to dinner, and he had to admit, Mrs. Werner's pot roast stood heads above the rest of the food he had eaten along his route, with perhaps the exception of Molly Redford's stewed rabbit. Small peas, lettuce leaves sprinkled with apple cider vinegar, corn—ripe as heaven could make it—and thick slices of tomato with cream and sugar. He wiped his mouth and rose to help clear the dishes.

"Oh, my, no, Preacher. You sit right there and wait for a big piece of my apple walnut cake and sweet cream. More coffee?"

"Ma'am, you'll have me so spoiled I won't want to ride out of here."

She smiled at his comment and pushed her daughter, Suzanna, forward with his cake and coffee. "Then maybe you should stay a spell longer." The insinuating gaze over her glasses told him to scream no and get away as fast as he could. No different than Mrs. Loiller. From now on when asked to dinner, he would inquire whether or not the family had courting-age daughters.

Mrs. Werner's daughter, an attractive girl, like all the others, held no special place in his heart. Oh, she had all the important things a young woman should have: laughing eyes, soft brown hair, a lively smile. But TJ didn't want any of that. He didn't want a woman in his life. Not at all, and if he did, she would have eyes darker than strong coffee, blond hair, a laughing smile, a… But he didn't want her. Not Suzanna, not Sarah, not Jeanette Loiller. He wanted them all to leave him alone.

He could not bring himself to be rude, however. "Now, Mrs. Werner, you tempt me sorely, but I do have families waiting on me in Gullywash. And we can't be selfish." He accepted the plate of cake sprinkled liberally with white sugar and cinnamon. "Thank you, Suzanna. I appreciate this fine meal. Your family has made me feel right at home."

Mrs. Werner didn't wait for her daughter to respond. "Suzanna prepared most of it, I must say. She's becoming quite the little homemaker. Make some lucky fellow a good wife one day." Her voice took on a nervous quaking when she spoke Suzanna's name and qualities. "And *such* a joy with the little ones. You remember how she plans their Sunday school lesson. She has a natural mother's way with children." She nudged Suzanna with her elbow. "Don't you, Suzanna, dear?"

Her husband groaned and gobbled at his piece of cake. "Let the man eat, wife. He has to be on his way." And then he mumbled something about "he'd better be if he knows what's good for him," but TJ didn't ask him to repeat it for clarity.

TJ smiled his appreciation for Mr. Werner's understanding, but Mrs. Werner's speech had just started. "Yes, she sews, as well. Knits, too, don't you, dear? My, last year she sewed Mr. Werner the finest wristlets and stockings you ever saw. Warm and cozy." She looked to her husband for confirmations. "Weren't they cozy, Mr. Werner? And the baby sweater for Caroline Jenkins's little one. Just precious. Precious as can be."

Mr. Werner grunted and slurped his coffee, his eyes never leaving his plate.

"Oh, Mama." Suzanna's face shone brighter than the apples they'd used for the cake, he was sure. And besides, after service he'd seen her and Orville Muriel holding hands by the swing at the side of the church, her face a blush of joy, his filled with hope. Did Mrs. Werner know about them? If so, she'd no doubt leave TJ alone and be standing with Suzanna on Orville's porch. With one push, Suzanna and Orville would be in need of TJ's services to marry them. But it wasn't up to TJ to tell tales out of school. Mrs. Werner would find out in good time.

When he rose to leave, Mrs. Werner placed a burlap bag in his hands. "Just a sandwich or two for the road. Maybe another piece of my cake?" Her eyebrows waggled up and down as he smiled at the offering. "And you go fill your canteen at the well. Water's good and deep, so you'll have a right cold drink and a supper to remember us by." She lingered over the words and winked at Suzanna. "All of us. Because we won't forget you, now, will we, Suzanna?"

"I thank you kindly, Mrs. Werner." He nodded to her husband and daughter. "I'll take my leave now."

Saul waited patiently at the front of the house, and TJ didn't spend as much time as usual stroking his long neck before rising into the saddle. Mrs. Werner had pushed her daughter to the porch, and she waved her hankie as if she were surrendering a battle. TJ laughed to himself and quickly mounted his horse. What a mother that woman was. A near-perfect copy of Mrs. Loiller. Worse yet, what a mother-in-law she would be one day. Poor Orville. Never mind what the daughter wanted. Another final wave and he tugged on Saul's reins, glad to hit the open road.

Molly and Sheriff Redford sounded mighty good. In two days he'd be back in Gullywash, and maybe he could put to rights all the mess he'd made before leaving last time.

Without realizing it, he began to whistle "Oh! Susanna," then laughed and kicked Saul's sides. *Hurry up, TJ, before the woman settles permanently into your brain or catches up to you in her wagon.*

Tuesday morning, the sun shone, full of promise for a perfect day. At least, that was what Sarah hoped as she put on her finest dress and cleaned Zach so he sparkled. "There you are, little man. Shiny as a penny."

His eyebrows knit together. "I'm a penny?" The questioning grin tugged her heart in many different directions.

Sarah clipped the edge of his chin. "Just means you're nice and clean and ready to go into town with me."

"What for, Mama?" Those simple words caused her

to ask herself the same. Would it make any difference in the end? Studdard was not going to help her.

Her good mood gone, Sarah's face burned with the anger she'd prayed all night for the Lord to take away, to no avail. Banker Studdard had better hope he was home with the grippe, because if he was in town, he had her to answer to once and for all.

"Candy?"

"Oh, no. Not today, young man. We have to save every bit of money. But you are going to visit Aunt Molly. Would you like that? Maybe she'll have some of her oatmeal cookies with walnuts."

"Cookies!" He jumped and clapped his hands.

"I have butter and eggs for you to give to her, all right?" At least she had that with all of her cluckers still on the farm. She had enough to give away and plenty to trade with Mrs. Haley.

He laughed and seemed unable to think of anything else but the cookies. Sarah hoped Molly had baked today.

The trip to town took forever, or rather, felt that way. Zach hollered about the cookies until Sarah had to speak sternly to him. Not fair to Zachary, but she couldn't stop her knees from shaking one against the other, so angry was she. She hadn't been this mad in her entire life. That vile banker. How dare he tell lies about her animals?

When at last she stopped at the Redfords', Zach jumped from the wagon. "Young man, are you forgetting something?"

"The eggs?"

Sarah tried to smile. "No. Your manners. Wait for Mama." She set the brake and picked up the box of eggs and butter.

Molly Redford walked out on the porch, shielding her eyes from the sun. "Oh, my. Who do we have here?"

"It's Zach, Aunt Molly." The sheriff's wife had told Sarah the last time they were in town that Zach might come for a visit anytime Sarah needed her help, and that Zach need not call her Mrs. Redford but Aunt Molly. Sarah appreciated the extra kindness. At least one family in town trusted her and cared about what happened to them.

"Say, there, young fella. How about an oatmeal cookie and some milk?"

Zach turned and grinned at Sarah in a knowing way. Then he whispered, "She has cookies, Mama. O-at-meal. Just like you said."

"You be on your best behavior, son. We can't have folks thinking we aren't polite."

"I will, Mama." He wasted little time waving; the cookies were in the house.

Molly frowned. "Why would anyone think that, Sarah Anne?"

She hung her head against her chest. Sarah felt a need to unburden herself. Tell Molly what the banker had done, but was that right? Then she would be a gossip, with folks thinking poorly of the man when she had no proof other than the word of the new farmer in town. Was he to be believed? No, her business was her business. Little sense in crying over what she couldn't change. "It's nothing, Molly. Sorry I had the weepies in front of you. Ever since the storm, well, my life has veered a bit from where I had expected it to go. Not all I'd planned, don't you know?"

"I'm sorry, Sarah. I wish we could do more to help."

"Not your responsibility. I owe you enough for

watching Zach. He talked about nothing but the possibility you'd baked this morning. I'm so grateful." She handed Molly the box. "See you later, Molly." And she headed toward the wagon, the weight of the whole world heavy on her shoulders. At least, that was how it felt to a woman about to lose her home.

Sarah dreaded the next task. Speaking with Banker Studdard. She gave Lightfoot a gentle scratch on the mane before climbing into the wagon. She clicked her tongue and Lightfoot headed back the way they'd come. Folks waved as she drove along, but a couple hung their heads and looked away. Perhaps they had heard she was trying to sell sick stock. She slapped the reins and in her mind she shot daggers at the banker.

She stopped the wagon for the second time, but this time with a mixture of anger and fear bubbling from her stomach to the top of her throat. What if he denied it? He could. But every one of the farmers, who she knew needed more animals, had turned her down. Then when Mr. Swenson admitted what Studdard had told him, the mean words had been too much. For Zach's sake as well as her own, she had to confront the cur. No self-respecting person would do any differently. She had a right to be heard.

Mr. Studdard's eyes opened wide when she marched into the bank, not taking a seat, not waiting for Mrs. Brekenridge to announce her, not offering a polite "Howdy do."

He immediately stood, surprise etched on his face. "Mrs. Rycroft. Won't you have a seat. Good to see you, my dear." His forehead speckled with sweat and it wasn't even hot outside.

"Good to see me? Good to see me?" She didn't sit.

She stood as tall as her petite frame would allow. "And don't you dare 'my dear' me. I have done everything I can to try and raise the money. All the while you were undermining me. How could you, Mr. Studdard?"

"I'm sure I don't know what you are talking about."

She made a fist at her side and wished she had brought her husband's Winchester. Maybe that would force the truth out of him. "You told all the farmers in the area that I have sick animals. You told them not to buy them."

He plunked into his seat, his face pale as the snow in winter. "You're mistaken, my de—"

"I have it on good authority that you spread rumors about my fine cows, pigs and chickens, not to mention my team of horses that Nathaniel raised and broke himself. You, Mr. Studdard, are doing your best to get my farm and I'd like to know why. I have not done one thing to harm another soul in this town. Never said an unkind word, before *or* after Nathaniel died. The fact is that I know you have given other folks longer to even up on their notes, and I haven't said a word against you. But still you do everything imaginable to harm me and my boy."

He stood and reached for her hand, but she pulled back faster than the blink of an eye. "Don't you touch me. No more phony consoling, Mr. Studdard. You stopped James from helping me, a good boy in spite of you, by the way, and I hear tell you told the men in town I didn't need help with the plowing. What else have you told folks that are out-and-out lies? A banker. A leader of our community who would stoop so low as a snake in the grass."

His teeth clamped together and his lips pursed into

a straight line. "I did you a favor, Mrs. Rycroft. You can't farm alone."

"You mean a woman."

"A woman? Yes, a woman has no business trying to farm on her own. I did you a favor. You should go home and thank me. Go back to Boston. Take your boy. Get him a good education. Find a man who will take care of you and the boy. You're acting foolish." He aimed a finger at the door. "Get out of my bank."

"I have every right to be here."

"What you have is until the end of September. After that your chance to save the the farm is off the table. Your foolishness has caused you to lose the profit you might have known from my sense of obligation. My generosity. Good day, Mrs. Rycroft!"

Myra Brekenridge gasped. The woman's frown followed Sarah out the door, but frowns of compassion couldn't save her farm.

Studdard shouted at her retreating footsteps. "I gave you an additional six months. I offered you a fair price. You've brought troubles on your own head, and your poor little fella will pay for your imprudence. You will rue this day, madam."

Sarah ran from the bank, head down, lips trembling. Barely able to lift her feet on the boardwalk, she ran smack into a wall of a man. She glanced up. TJ O'Brien grabbed her shoulders and caught her before she fell. "Sarah? Are you all right?"

"Mr. O'Brien. Oh, I'm sorry." She stood tall, her chin jutting forward. No sense sharing the bad news with the whole world. "I didn't see you there."

"What's happened? You're upset." His face creased into concern, looking more handsome than she'd remembered. *Foolish thought. Go away. This is no time to think about the man's face. You're losing your farm, not courting the preacher.*

"Oh, I'm fine," she lied. "And how was your trip this month?" As he helped her into her wagon, she took his hand and tingling warmth skittered across her palm. Could he tell what she was thinking? He must have heard the banker yelling at her. Her humiliation hadn't ended in the bank; the whole town must have listened to the encounter.

TJ's gaze narrowed on her. "A more difficult trip than usual. Mrs. Merriman is having a hard time letting go of..."

"You can say it, Mr. O'Brien. Her husband." Her lip quivered, her breath caught in her throat and with that, Sarah crumpled against the seat, tears coursing down her face. "He said no." She could do nothing to stop the sobs. If she were truly a good woman, she'd be comforting him. He had just said he'd had a difficult trip. At the very least, he certainly didn't need her adding to his problems.

His face clouded. "Who said no? What's wrong, Sarah?" He climbed into the wagon and sat next to her. "Here. Let's drive out of town so you may have some privacy." He clucked to the horse and the wagon rolled forward.

It came to rest under a little copse of trees where they could share words without prying eyes. Sarah gulped each breath, feeling every bit *the widow woman with troubles*.

"Tell me, Sarah. Who has upset you?"

She drew in a deep breath, doing her best to calm herself, but nothing helped. Sarah turned to face the preacher and collapsed against his shoulder, where she immediately found solace in his warmth. "The banker! He's been telling lies about my livestock. I tried to sell them to get enough money to make good on the note."

"He lied. To whom?"

"To all the farmers in the area. I don't know how or when, but he must have known I'd try to sell the stock. And he told folks my animals were sick. What kind of person does that? Isn't he one of your churchgoers? And you wonder why I don't go to God with my problems. A bunch of hypocrites is who you preach to—that's all you have in your church. A God who doesn't care and townsfolk who want me gone."

"Everyone isn't like that."

She thought of Molly and Sheriff Redford, who had brought TJ to town. "No, I don't suppose they are."

He cradled her against his shoulder, all the time gazing into her face. "Surely he'll allow you more time." He tipped her chin up with his thumb but let go in a hurry.

"He said I have until the end of September. Not a day more. Oh, TJ, what will I do? I can't go back home. I can't! And no one will buy my animals with the rumors he spread."

TJ held her in his arms, her head resting below his chin. The smell of lavender tickled his nose and he remembered the sweet-smelling soap he'd washed up with at her house. A good smell, better than the pine soap he used. A smell he'd missed in his travels.

What was he thinking? He had his arms full of Sarah Anne Rycroft and he should be consoling her, not thinking about how wonderful she smelled. But he drew in another breath. Then, with gentle fingers, he pushed the hair back beneath her bonnet. Pulling a hankie from his pocket, he smudged the moisture from her eyes. "No one's going to send you back home. I'll talk to the banker if needs be. We'll find a way."

"No! You can't." Her eyes opened wide with...what? Fear? He could talk to Studdard and he would. After all, Studdard was one of his flock, as was Sarah, and he ought to be able to make the man see the sense in helping a widow. But the man had lied about Sarah. A Christian man who was supposed to have a conscience. More likely a greedy man with no principles. That simply could not be allowed. A man of the church, a pillar of their community. Shameful behavior.

His gaze dropped to the back of the wagon. "Where's Zach?" He shook her shoulders. "Sarah. Where's Zachary?"

She glanced up, tears still pooling in those beautiful dark eyes of hers. "He's at Molly Redford's." She sniffed and mumbled something about cookies.

"Well, you can't see the boy like this. You'll frighten him with your tears."

She stiffened. "I'm *not* crying."

With a smile, he said, "All right, you're not crying. Then let's not allow him to see you this angry. That would upset him even more. You're a kind and gentle woman, Sarah Anne, and I don't want your son to see you so heated." There, that word shouldn't upset her further.

"And I'm not heated, either." Sarah turned her face into his chest once again. "I...am...not." And the tears continued to trail over his buttons.

He patted her back, consoling not exactly being his best ability, but since he'd known her, he was learn-

ing. And he wasn't exactly averse to the feelings that
rippled through him at her touch. "All right, now." He
lifted her face and choked back the lump in his throat.
The tears sparkled in her eyes like diamonds. Chocolate
diamonds. Was there such a thing? In front of him...
there was.

She murmured, "Let's go get Zach."

"We should have you wash your face so you'll be
feeling better before you pick him up. While you go to
the Redfords', I'll speak with the banker." He held up
his palm. "No. I *will* speak with him, Sarah." In spite of
all his good intentions of a life free of family and worry,
TJ wanted nothing more than to crush her against him
and kiss away her sadness. Let her know he'd see her
through all her troubles, big and small, for the rest of
their lives. But he scarcely took care of himself. No
home. No place for him to establish a church where
he could preach every week. And even if he wanted to
take on her problems as his own, he hadn't ever kissed
a woman before. Didn't have a starting point. Well,
the occasional peck on the cheek to let old ladies know
he cared about their sorrows; that was all. TJ gazed at
Sarah's full pink lips and shuddered all the way down
his body to his boots, as if all sense of self-control had
flown away with the last crow. He wanted to kiss her.
He really wanted to. And kiss her good!

But he couldn't. He'd never kissed a woman before,
not a woman like...Sarah Anne.

Chapter 10

TJ swallowed the words he wanted to say to Mr. Studdard. He was as riled as a cornered snake when he approached the bank, but showing his anger wouldn't get him any closer to helping Sarah. Might just upset the man more. So he drew in a deep breath, held it and released it slowly so that his heart didn't pump so hard in his chest.

He greeted Myra Brekenridge with a forced smile and noticed old Ezra Milton, another of his flock. A man who had started a family very late in life, and one of the farmers Sarah said she had approached.

"Good day to you, Mr. Milton."

The man held out a well-callused hand. "And to you, Preacher. Guess we'll all be meetin' in the bank hereabouts after that storm took all our crops away from us. Day after day I find another problem only Mr. Studdard and money can fix."

TJ nodded. "You lost your crop, too, then? I'm very sorry." He raised his voice a tad for the banker's sake. "Looks like every one of us will be pitching in to help one another this year, won't we? I heard you were looking for a milch cow for the young'uns."

"I, uh... Well, yes. I did want a good milker. You know of anybody with one to sell? Cheap?"

"Sarah Rycroft has two cows and two calves she'd part with, right reasonable. I spoke with her a few minutes ago, as a matter of fact. Good sound stock."

Milton stepped closer. He put a hand over his mouth and whispered low so only TJ could hear, "I heard tell they was sick. Studdard said she's trying to sell animals that's no good. I can't afford to spend money on a sick cow at a time like this."

TJ glared at the banker and raised his voice. "Is that so? Now, I've seen those animals myself. They look mighty healthy to me. Who'd you say was passing 'round rumors about Mrs. Rycroft's animals?"

Studdard's eyes glared at TJ, but he refused to back off. He leaned his arms on his desk and pushed forward, gaze leveled at TJ without so much as a blink.

"I'm mighty sorry, Mr. O'Brien. Just can't take a chance on unhealthy cattle. Money's too scarce at the moment."

TJ turned his attention back to Milton. "You gonna make it with your note?"

"Indeed," Mr. Milton said. "We'll have to." He stood close again and looked around to see if Studdard was listening in. "If it weren't for another extension on my note, I'd lose my entire farm. But Studdard's all wool and a yard wide. Ready and willing to help me keep my property but says I can't risk any of his loan on animals that might be sick. So, you see, if he says them animals is no good, them animals is no good. I don't have much choice but to listen to him or he'll deny me the money. You see what I'm sayin', Preacher? My family depends on me to get us out of debt."

TJ's hand molded into fists at his side. Was this how Peter felt when confronted by folks talking ill of the Savior? He could see it now. Or when Jesus himself stepped into the den of thieves at the temple. That was it. "Is that how it goes? I've walked into a den of thieves? And here I thought I was in the bank."

From across the room, face as purple as a wild flag on the riverbank, the banker looked directly at TJ, understanding exactly why he was here. At last he moved around the desk in front and held out his hand. Always with the appearance of a gentleman. But TJ didn't shake the offered hand. "Well, now. Good to see you back, Preacher. We need a few sound words to help us along in these trying times. Been a difficult few weeks in Gullywash." TJ pictured a Pharisee. All that was missing was a long robe and tall hat. So that was why Sarah saw hypocrites in his flock. And Banker Studdard a fine example of Christian charity, doing everything he could to throw Sarah and her boy from their own farm.

With a smirk that set TJ's teeth to grinding, Studdard said, "We have a mite more trouble today than usual, that's a fact."

"We do that, Mr. Studdard. One reason I'm here is because of all the troubles we all, as good stewards of charity, share. You know, helping one another in these *times*." He gave his best Uncle Michael frown. "With a few good words to help things along. Mr. Studdard, we need to talk."

Studdard stopped gaping, his brows shooting up. "Myra, a cup of coffee for our friend here." He indicated a chair next to his desk in the back. "Please, have a seat. You are always welcome here, Mr. O'Brien."

TJ shifted in the seat to show himself as tall and sturdy, as menacing, as possible. He might come with love in one hand, but righteous anger wasn't far from the other.

"I'll cut to the chase, Mr. Studdard. I'm here on behalf of Sarah Rycroft." The banker stood. TJ waved him down by pointing at the chair with all the control he could muster and a dose of *no nonsense, if you please.* "Sit down, Mr. Studdard, and hear me out. You've been a busy ant where Mrs. Rycroft is concerned. I'm sure you've heard that the Lord detests lying lips, but He delights in men who are truthful. That's Proverbs 12:22 in case you've been a bit remiss in reading your Bible verses in these *troubled times.* You know that verse, Mr. Studdard?"

A couple snickers drifted from the front of the bank, where more townsfolk had gathered, but TJ didn't bother with them. Studdard did. He eyed Milton and Mrs. Brekenridge, indicating he'd tolerate no nonsense. But TJ believed Studdard deserved whatever he got from this conversation, so he refused to lower his voice. He might feel bad later if he chose, bad enough to get down on his knees to ask for forgiveness, but right now he had a plan of action and nothing would deter him.

Suddenly pale with all the folks staring at him, Studdard's voice cracked. "I—I'm a business man, Mr. O'Brien, and I don't appreciate you preaching to me in m-my place of business. You have no right." He eased from his chair, but TJ rose and pressed him back into it, his hand digging into Studdard's shoulder to hold him in place.

His size, compared to the banker, was a definite advantage in this confrontation. "Do you think God stops watching because you come into work? He doesn't all of a sudden wake up on Sunday morning and say He's going to see what Banker Studdard is doing. He watches over us *every* day. Every day, Mr. Studdard. He knows all of our actions as well as our words."

Studdard regained his bravado. "And I suppose He would approve of you browbeating the town banker. Is that what preachers do now, Mr. O'Brien? Go about frightening their flocks?"

"No. I don't suppose He will be happy with me about it, but that's between me and the Lord. It has little to do with you. It's my obligation to watch over all my folks. Let 'em know when they're headed over a cliff. I may have to ask for a good healthy dose of forgiveness when I leave here, but you—" he pointed at Studdard "—should be on your knees right now. Not waiting to go home. Right now, Studdard. And if you plan to join your wonderful family in eternity one day, you'd better start thinking about how you treat folks today. Every day."

"Why, I never."

"Probably not. You still won't answer my question?"

"If it's about Mrs. Rycroft, no."

TJ pulled his hat from his head and rifled fingers through his damp hair. "So you won't make an effort at all to help Sarah?"

"Sarah, is it?"

TJ knew better than to engage in that conversation. "Other than spread lies about *Mrs.* Rycroft's animals, that is?"

"There's nothing you can say. I have no idea who is spreading rumors, and her note falls due end of the month. I told Mrs. Rycroft that this morning. Less than a week and she'll have to even up. She's already been granted an extension. I have the other folks who put money in my bank to think of. Anything else would be wasteful. A woman farmer indeed. Well, my hands are tied. There will be no extension for the Rycroft farm."

TJ's skin crawled being in the same room with the man—a man who'd warmed his seat in church every Sunday since TJ had come to town. And yet here he was, ready to turn a woman and her boy out of her home. "Are they, now? I've heard tell other folks have been granted second and third extensions."

"Well…with a male head of the house."

TJ chewed the edge of his lip. He should come right out and say what was on his mind. "Is that really the issue, Mr. Studdard? A male head of the house? Or is it that you can turn a nice profit at her expense?"

Studdard's face paled instantly, then slowly turned from bright red to purple. Like an oversize eggplant with jowls flapping in frustration, he rose to his feet. And TJ had his answer.

In no time, his heart for the lost took over. *Remember, he, too, is a child of God.*

I might remember, but I don't have to like it.

Then that quiet word shot straight to his heart—again. *Trust. How do I trust a Pharisee, Lord? Trust.* Deep in his heart, this time, the word sank.

Trust and show compassion for Studdard.

Not even realizing what he was doing, TJ held out his hand, which nearly floored the banker. Surprised TJ, too. "Thank you, sir, for hearing me out. I'll show myself to the door. Do me a favor and think about what I said. Just think about it."

Studdard slumped back into his chair with a thunk. "I'll think on it. For your sake, not Sarah Rycroft's."

TJ dropped a grin in Myra's direction and gave a short salute to the other people waiting in the bank. "Good day to you, ma'am. Folks."

She held her hand over her chest, her face pale as a turnip. "Yes, sir. Mighty fine day. We're happy you came to town, Preacher."

Mumbling a great deal under his breath, TJ smiled all the way out the door. His steps took him across the street and into the sheriff's office. The minute he entered, his human nature took over once again, and he punched the wall...hard.

"Meeting went that well, did it?"

"What?" Hand to his mouth, TJ nursed three sore knuckles. He slipped a hankie from his pocket and pressed it against his fingers.

Redford slid his feet from his desk and cut to the chase. "Listen, I figured you'd go talk to Studdard. But, TJ, he won't budge. He wants to turn Sarah out. Lock, stock and barrel."

"I didn't think for one minute that man would give Sarah Anne the time of day, let alone an extension on her note. I hear things. And I'm thinking Studdard wants the property for a deal with someone else. He's bent over backward to help other families with their notes, but for some reason, he just won't help Sarah. Unless it's a money matter, why is she the only one?"

Redford nodded. "Her land is good. That wheat would have cleared all her debt and then some. Nathaniel Rycroft was one capable farmer."

"Sarah's capable herself."

"Don't get riled. I agree. I didn't mean to make light of what she's done out there." The sheriff slapped his hat on his head and adjusted his gun belt, apparently making ready to go home for lunch. "But Nathaniel had a way with the land. Every bit of manure his farm produced went into the soil, and when we had a late snow three years ago, he plowed it under. 'Poor man's fertilizer,' he called it." He slapped TJ on the shoulder and guided him out of the office. Once on the board-walk, he shot a withering look in the bank's direction. "Yes, sir, Nathaniel Rycroft had a way with the land, all right. Richest land in these parts when he started, and he made it even richer. Makes a man sort of wonder, now, doesn't it?"

"I hate to think ill of Mr. Studdard," TJ said, "but it does appear odd he goes after only Sarah's property like this."

"Let's go have us a sandwich. Molly has leftover roast that I'm praying will be my dinner. We can talk over the suspicions about Studdard."

They both cocked a grin at Studdard's boy as he stroked Saul's neck and fed him an apple. What an up-standing young man. Nothing like his father. "Hey, Preacher. Thought he might like an apple. Hope it's all right."

"Hey, yourself. I guess you won't spoil him much." The boy was not exactly the acorn fallen from the tree.

Zach had gone outside to play with his marbles, but still Sarah spoke softly to Molly so he wouldn't over-hear. "I have nothing else to sell. All the rumors about my animals have made it impossible to sell so much as a chicken. I have to wonder if Mrs. Haley will continue to buy my eggs and butter if all the folks believe what's being said." She stared at her finger for a moment. "All I have left is my ring from Nathaniel. And I don't seem to be able to part with it. Maybe between the ring and my father's gold pocket watch, I'd have enough for Studdard to give me till spring. I've cried myself out and that does no one any good." All she had left…a few sniffles here and there.

Molly frowned and stopped slicing the beef in front of her on the table. "Lands, don't you even consider selling that ring. We simply need to put our heads together. Surely one of us will come up with an idea. You and the boy stay for dinner. Mr. Redford and I will be pleased to have you. No more talk about you two going back east. We'd miss that boy of yours something fierce. And the city to raise a young fella? Why, that's unheard of. You two need us like we need you. And we all need Gullywash."

"I'm aware of that. You don't have to convince me that the city isn't a great place." A smile tipped Sarah's lips. And Zach would miss the sheriff and Molly. Without family around, they had become like grandparents to him. And they loved children. "We'd both miss you. You've been kinder than words can say. Of course we'll find a way to stay. Thank you. And for dinner."

She dried the last tear as in walked Sheriff Redford and…TJ O'Brien.

Dinner was overall very quiet. Redford and his wife did their best to hold up their leg of the conversation, but Sarah seemed overly subdued. Not Zach, though.

"Did you know ladybugs is red?"

"Yes." Molly laughed.

"Did you know bees can sting, but they make honey?"

"Sweet as anything," the sheriff replied.

"Why's grass all green and flowers has colors?"

Sarah smiled. "Because that's the way God made them."

TJ quirked a brow.

"Why do you mens has guns?

The sheriff nodded. "To protect our property and our families."

And the last took the wind out of TJ's belly. "We can't get candy 'cause Mama's saving all her pennies for the man at the bank. Why's he want Mama's pennies? Can't he get pennies of his own?"

Sarah's face fell, an expression of humiliation covering her otherwise beautiful features. How he wished he'd been successful when he'd visited the bank. Anything that would wipe the frown from Sarah's beautiful face.

TJ grinned. "There just might be one piece of candy at the store that has your name on it. What do you think, young man?"

"It does? I dinnunt see my name on the candy."

Everyone laughed at Zach's comment. TJ wanted to hug the boy to his chest and tell him there would be lots of candy with his name on it one day, but he couldn't be sure of that. No sense in lying to the boy when he didn't know how the banknote would end up. Uncle Michael had always been honest with TJ, all except about the money from his folks. He hadn't known until the day Uncle Michael gave it to him. All his uncle's hardships, and still he hadn't used the money intended for TJ's future.

When the coffee was passed a second time and Molly had served them all a large wedge of gingerbread with a dollop of whipped cream, TJ turned to Sarah. "I have a proposition I'd like to make concerning the plowing." His fork cut into the tender gingerbread, and he heaved a sigh when he tasted it along with the drop of cream.

"You what?" Her eyes met his, and he swallowed hard as he melted into them. His heart hammered at her words. He licked his lips, catching her gaze.

Chiding himself, he started over. "I thought perhaps you could use some help with the plowing. I know this man."

"Just any man?"

"Well, how about me? I don't do all that much between services, and if I stayed in Gullywash a couple extra weeks…"

She shook her head. "But I have no money to pay you, and just because you're a preacher doesn't mean you do things for folks for nothing. There's a line that's drawn and you needn't worry yourself about my plowing."

"Can't friends step over the line even if they are preachers?"

"But I can't pay you." Sarah's face had a woebegone look about it, and he longed to be able to soothe her. Let her know the money didn't really matter, but she wouldn't believe that. Wouldn't be able to understand it. Shucks, he didn't understand all these feelings swirling around in his head himself. He'd made a promise and never considered wavering…until Sarah Anne and Zach.

"No, Sarah, you're right. I have to eat, as well, but what if we strike a bargain? I'll send word I'm going to stay longer in Gullywash this week. Maybe two weeks. I'll help you with the plowing. You'll feed me, of course, but then I'll have some sweat invested in the crop. Come next spring, you can pay me when the crop comes in."

She leaned her arm on the table and spoke quietly, "And if I don't get this crop in, either?"

"Then we both lose. Together. But I said *when* the crop comes in, not *if.*"

She shook her head, looked at Zach hopefully, and TJ could tell he'd tempted her. After all, it was fair. He would be taking the same chance on the crop that she was.

Molly poured more coffee, patting Sarah's hand as she went. "Sarah. Sounds like a good bargain to me. Let the man help you. Don't be prideful. He's offering honest work for honest pay. When you reap a good crop, he makes money along with you." Her eyes twinkled. "Not that it's any of my business, mind you."

"And if the crop fails? I've failed so much since Nathaniel died."

A loud sigh escaped TJ's lips. "You haven't failed, Sarah. Remember, the rain falls on the worthy and the unworthy. So it stands to reason that bad things also happen to the good folks as well as the bad. I'll take my chances along with you. If the crop's a mighty fine one, then I'll have money to begin to build a real church in this town. We won't have to meet in the saloon anymore. I can't tell you how happy *that* would make me."

They all laughed, knowing what a thorn it was in everyone's side to have to meet in a saloon. "You see what I mean? None of us wants to be meeting there."

Redford added, "And you both understand how it galls me. I see 'em on Sunday and lock 'em up the following Saturday night. Although I shouldn't really complain. At least some of those same folks stick around for the service in a place not foreign to them."

TJ couldn't stop the excitement he felt at the idea of a church for the town. "And we could use it as a school during the week as well as a church on Sunday. "Wouldn't it be wonderful to have all the students in a schoolhouse instead of taking lessons at home and with tutors?" He slapped his hands together. "The more I think of it, you'd be doing the town a favor. And for what? A few days' work."

"A few days? Have you seen my fields?"

He nodded and smiled. "Yes, I have. There is plenty of good vegetation to be plowed under. Your cows still producing manure?"

Sarah laughed, a hearty, happy laugh, for the first time the entire meal. "They are, and so are the chickens and horses. In abundance."

"Then I reckon with my sturdy legs and your manure, we have a good chance at a good crop. What do you say? Will you let me be part of all that money you're going to be raking in next spring?"

Chapter 11

Unable to sleep, Sarah went through her personal items one last time as if by some miracle another precious object would appear that she could sell and turn into cash for the banker. But in truth, the only property she still owned that might bring her money was her ring and her father's gold pocket watch, all she had left of both of the important men in her life. There was the lamp, but no one would pay good money for a well-used lamp.

She fell to her knees, the watch and ring clutched in her fingers. *Father, I have these two things to sell. Please find me the right person to buy them, and please...please let me get the price I need. I thank you for holding me up when I wanted to quit. But even if I can't get the money, I'm yours, now. Forever. No more bargains, no more loving You only in the good times. Forgive me, Father. Forgive my stubborn pride.*

Instead of feeling an overwhelming sadness, Sarah's heart filled with joy when she realized the ring and watch themselves didn't mean that much. The memories of her father and Nathaniel were what mattered. And while she would have loved to pass the objects on to Zach, the farm had to be saved. For both of their sakes. The farm would go to Zach when he grew up. It would be the only reminder of how his father had worked hard to provide for him. And passing that along would give him more of a sense of accomplishment than a piece of gold.

Who might need a ring and a pocket watch, she wasn't sure, but someone might. And Thursday she was determined to strike the sale.

She rose up from the floor and glanced toward the window; the sky had begun to lighten a bit. Must be at least five. She had to hurry and wash up, fix breakfast and get ready for work. TJ O'Brien would be here at six to start on the fields. Hot coffee and biscuits had to be waiting as part of the bargain. At least, as far as she was concerned.

Saul nipped at TJ's fingers, begging for an apple. TJ rubbed the horse's velvety ears and whispered to him, "You are getting spoiled, fella. That James Studdard surely does appreciate good horse flesh, but you'll be as big as you are tall if he doesn't quit sneaking you treats." Then he smoothed the big bay's neck and drew the bit into Saul's mouth in one fluid motion. As he finished cinching the saddle, his thoughts wandered to the brown eyes that had crept into his dreams last night. The same eyes that had kept him from sleeping soundly the past two months.

"I'm mighty fond of that lady, fella. But you can't tell anyone. Not even me. Because I made a promise a long time ago. One I plan to keep. The good Lord has honored me all these years, and now I have to honor Him. Can't let my thoughts wander around to the lady. It wouldn't be right." Still, the dreams didn't stop. He tried to pray his feelings away, wish them away, force them away, but Sarah's brown eyes found him each night when his head hit the feather pillow in Molly's guest room. Found him, lassoed him, pulled him into their embrace.

He sighed, huge enough that it felt it would rip his chest apart. He must look like a lovesick fool around Sarah, and he'd be happy to see love reflected in her eyes, but that wasn't likely. He'd made a promise and promises were meant to be kept. He owed his entire life to God. A bargain was a bargain.

"Let's go, Saul. You and me are going to have a long ride and then put in a good day's work. At least, I am. You'll be lollygagging in the paddock not earning your keep." He hoped Lightfoot could pull a plow, because Saul had been tried in harness only once before and TJ found, as he'd suspected, Saul wasn't suited to it.

Sarah swatted Zach on the seat of his pants and shooed him out the door. "Stay close, you hear?"

"One more biscuit, please?"

She handed him another biscuit, and he promised to go feed Sassy the rest of his milk.

"No wasting. You drink your milk till you're full, then give kitty the rest."

"I will." He skipped out the door with Sassy's dish in one hand and his crumbly biscuit in the other.

"Don't spill," she shouted after the fading footsteps. "Hi, Mis-ter O'Brien."

Zach no sooner cleared the doorway than a huge shadow passed. "Mornin', ma'am."

As TJ removed his hat, Sarah noticed a spike of black hair at the back of his head, and she wanted to smooth it down, but he reached up and flattened it when he ran his fingers through from front to back. That had saved her from making a complete fool of herself.

He looked different somehow. That was it. No black jacket and long coat. He was in work pants, shirt, suspenders and boots. But still handsome in an earthy way. A way that fluttered her stomach.

She worried the edge of her lip. "Good morning, Mr. O'Brien. Your breakfast is ready."

"Sarah, I thought we'd got past the Mr. and Mrs. a long time—"

"Mr. and Mrs.?" Her face must have turned a dozen shades of red and more as she stuttered to put things right. "Oh, certainly. Of course. I, uh… Yes, TJ, you're correct. We did say we didn't need formality. Here's your coffee." She rushed forward with a cup and then felt more the fool. "I mean, here. Sit down. I have biscuits, wild berry jam and coffee all ready for you."

His lips tipped at the edges and she didn't know what to say to make things better.

She poured herself a cup and bowed her head to take her mind off his smile.

"Amen." TJ smelled the rich coffee and biscuits but didn't seem to be able to lift his head. Had she prayed over the food? He opened one eye to discover her with a full smile, all the way to the crinkles at the corners of her eyes.

Her words tempered his heart. "Good Lord gave us a mighty fine day to start the plowing."

"He did that." What had happened since he'd left her in the field the night of the storm? "And I don't see a cloud in the sky." He slathered a biscuit with jam and licked his lips after the first bite. "These are fine biscuits. Did you make the jam?"

"Glad you like them. And, yes, I did. Zach loves jam on his biscuits." What was it about that smile on her face? On her beautiful face? He could count the times he'd seen her smile on one hand until now.

"By the way, Lightfoot has plowed before, right?" He finished the second biscuit and swigged the last drops of coffee. When she started to pour more, he held up his hand. "No, thank you. Lightfoot?"

"Yes, she plows. More than the roans, but they're used to harness, as well, if we need them. Nathaniel said they were too spry for the harness, so he used Lightfoot."

"Good. I doubt Saul would be much help."

"Good, then." Her gaze traveled over him when he stood.

"Well, if you'll show me the way, I'd like to get started."

While TJ harnessed Lightfoot, Sarah finished her chores, still mortified by her unladylike behavior. She'd been gawking at him like some saloon girl.

Once she had recovered, she'd checked on Zach and cleaned up the breakfast mess. She started a large pot of soup from a leftover piece of beef that Molly had sent home with her. She cleaned and cut up carrots, two ears of corn and a fresh pot of beans. Potatoes from the cellar and an onion finished the soup. After she put it on to simmer slowly until noon, she drew a bucket of water from the well and added some apple cider vinegar and a bit of honey to sweeten it. Though she'd humiliated herself at breakfast, she couldn't allow her embarrassment to prevent TJ from a morning break.

Adding an apple to her pocket for Lightfoot, Sarah hurried into the field with the bucket and a ladle. At the edge, she stopped in wonder. He'd plowed a good eighth of the field already. And though he was sweating like a house afire, he and Lightfoot didn't seem any worse for wear.

"Whoa." He slowed Lightfoot, then brought her to a stop. "What have we here?"

Sarah held her breath. Nathaniel had used the same expression. How alike they were and yet different in so many ways. She smiled. This man was helping her to keep her farm alive; she had no plans to waste her time dwelling on the past at the moment. "How would you like some vinegar water?"

"If you made it plenty sweet, I'd like it fine."

"I do believe all you men like it sweet."

He grinned as she stirred the water in the bucket.

Again? When would she learn to curb her tongue? "You know good and well what I meant." She gulped and bit the edge of her cheek. Why had she said that? His eyes were twinkling and a fresh wave of humiliation whirled over her.

TJ reached for the ladle and drank deep of the good water. "Perfect, Sarah. Just what a man needs to stave off the thirst." His gaze lingered a bit too long on her mouth. "Something sweet. And is that apple for me, too?"

"No." She lifted the apple to Lightfoot's mouth. With one huge crunch, the fruit was gone. "I think she deserves the apple more than you. You're fresh."

He winked. "Thank you, Sarah." Then he replaced the ladle and gazed over the field. "Say, I haven't seen Zach much this morning. Where is he?"

Sarah placed the bucket on the ground. "He 'helpded' Sassy catch a mouse this morning. Sassy's sleeping off the meal, and Zach's sleeping off the excitement. He came in for a nap right after the big kill. You would have thought he had a lion on his shoulder instead of a mouse by the tail. I can't believe Sassy let him handle it, but she did. And then he gave it back to her to eat. They are quite the pair. Great hunters."

TJ chuckled and tugged his hat over his brow again so he could get back to work. The man had eyes that could see right through a body. Sarah shivered in spite of the fact the heat rippled in waves over the freshly plowed earth. She leaned down and sifted dirt through her fingers. How could she ever repay him for plowing the wheat field?

Slapping the reins to put life into Lightfoot, TJ raised a hand in mock salute. "Back to work, captain."

Sarah lifted the bucket again. "I'll leave this in the shade for you." Moisture covered the fabric stretching over TJ's well-muscled back. She licked her lips and quickly downed a ladle of the good cold water. With the air terribly warm and sticky today, she had trouble putting her mind back on the farm. She had no time, and certainly no inclination, to think more of the preacher than a friend. Best she returned to her own chores and left him to do his.

But she didn't miss a chance to take another peek at his broad shoulders.

TJ eyed the row next to him to be sure and keep a straight line, but when he heard the soft footfalls behind him, he simply had to turn around and watch Sarah stroll back to the house. She tripped over one of the rows, and he waited to be certain she was all right. Not sure whether all this plowing was going to do any good—she could still lose the farm to the bank—he had to wonder why he had offered to turn over the fields. Maybe he had to in order to stay positive. Or maybe he couldn't resist that look of lost little girl in her eyes. The look in her eyes that dared him to help her in spite of her words to the contrary.

She reminded him of young Mrs. McEnnery, whose babes had died. She had been only twenty-one years old with four young children, another on the way, when she, her husband and children had arrived in New York City. And though she'd lost three babes to scarlet fever, she was in the family way again when TJ had left to go west. He prayed their lives had grown easier somehow, but he doubted it. Now here was Sarah with that familiar look of one who had known too much hardship in her short life.

He shook his head, cleared his mind. *Keep your thoughts where they belong...on the field. No need to make more of this than a business partnership.*

Into his head crept the image of Zach and the kitten catching a mouse. He laughed out loud until Lightfoot swished her tail. She might as well have said, "Get back to work, Preacher."

As the image of the boy grew clearer, TJ scratched the back of his neck. This had to stop. He was here for one reason only. He was a preacher helping a widow, albeit a beautiful young widow, to keep her farm.

That *was* it, wasn't it?

Chapter 12

Wednesday morning. Two days left to even up on the note.

The time had finally arrived, and Sarah knew what steps she must take. No miracles had arrived with the cavalry. No word from the banker that he'd changed his mind. She had to try the last hope she had.

She twisted the ring on her finger. As it moved up and down, the white band of skin underneath and slight indentation spoke to the amount of time the ring had been on her finger—she had never taken it off. Never. Could she do this?

Nathaniel would expect her to move on with her life. But could she sell the ring he had put on her hand seven years ago when they married and headed west? Even if it meant saving the farm?

She walked to the front door and opened it. A rush of

clean, fresh air filled her nostrils. While this farm had been Nathaniel's dream, it had soon become hers. The first time she watched Zach, arms flapping and hair ruffling in the breeze, chasing a "chickie" across the grass, she knew a child should be raised in the country, better yet, in the West, where open spaces and clear air would fill his heart and mind forever. Her gaze drifted to the front of the porch. Wild roses and herbs grew side by side. Lemon verbena, mint and chamomile filled the air with their own special scents. Sarah breathed deeply.

This was her farm now. Not Banker Studdard's, not even Nathaniel's. Hers and Zach's. She slapped her palm on the porch rail. And by gum, with the help of the good Lord, she aimed to keep it!

Sarah walked back inside and listened to Zach shifting around in bed, talking in his sleep as he did every morning before waking up. Walking to his door, she continued swirling the ring like a dance on her finger. She looked at his sweet baby face and pulled on her gold band. She could do it. For Zach she could do anything, no matter how painful.

"You have enough to eat, young man?"

TJ smiled at Molly Redford. "Between you and Sarah Anne, Saul's going to want me to shed a few pounds. I finish here and she has biscuits and coffee for me every morning when I get to the farm."

Molly's eyebrow rose in a telling way, so TJ quickly added, "Though this morning I doubt she will. I'm running late. She'll crack the whip and make me hop to it. Only there to get the plowing done. Nothing else."

Molly waved him away with her hand. "Oh, pshaw! Young fella like you workin' that field like you are can't get enough meat on your bones. You let me spoil you just a bit. I miss my boys bein' here, and if that means a boarder to cook for, then so be it. I enjoy cooking for company."

"If I'm company, then I've probably been here long enough. Worn out my welcome." He laughed, happy the conversation had steered away from Sarah.

"You are right at that. I guess I can't call you company anymore." Molly stepped toward him with more coffee and pinched one of his cheeks as if he were three years old. "You're like one of my own boys now. And if truth be told, Sarah and the boy are like my own, as well. Now, isn't *that* just convenient?"

He waited for her to finish pouring. "Right happy that you think so, ma'am." She was acting like the mothers in the other towns. When would she start telling him what a wonderful cook and mother Sarah was?

"You know," Molly said, "she's a right good cook and a wonderful mother, too. Any man would be lucky to have her for a wife. Don't you think so, TJ?"

Once the last drops of that good coffee were finished, TJ didn't waste any more time. He trudged out back to saddle Saul. Rubbing the big bay's neck and giving him an extra handful of oats, he thought about his promise to God. Had he promised not to have a personal life? How could he be sure exactly what God made of the promise? Plenty of preachers had wives; look at Mrs. Merriman. She and her husband had apparently lived a wonderful life, together *and* for the Lord. But Preacher Merriman hadn't promised God his whole life. Or had he? What constituted a man's entire life?

Saul whooshed and pushed at the hand rubbing his muzzle. TJ chuckled. "You are the bossy one, aren't you?" He slapped him along the neck with sure strokes. "What would I do without you, boy? You have been my most faithful companion since I was barely old enough to be out here alone."

Once in the saddle, he nudged Saul forward. The sun wasn't up yet, but the sky had started to lighten and cast a pink haze through the clouds. God's country. Free and beautiful.

As he turned out of the sheriff's onto the street, he waved a hand at James Studdard. "Mornin', boy."

"Mornin', Preacher. Off to work, I see."

TJ stopped alongside the banker's son. "Yes, more plowing to do. Say, what happened to you helping Mrs. Rycroft anyway? I thought you worked for her every chance you got. Saving up your money, your pa said."

"Yeah, well." The boy stepped closer and looked around. "Mr. O'Brien. You tell her I'm real sorry about not helping. My pa's got a burr in his tack for some reason when it comes to that poor lady. He said I couldn't work out there anymore. And—" he gazed about another time "—I heard him tell two men in the bank the other day that he'd heard she didn't need any help this fall. I don't know why, but he doesn't seem to care much for her. I think she's a fine woman. Always treated me fair and all. Paid me what I was worth, even last spring when the money was scarce, she gave me a pig and knew I'd be able to sell it for more than she owed me."

"She is fair at that," TJ agreed.

"Well, I'd best get ready for school or Pa'll tan my hide. He says it don't matter how old I get, he'll take me out back if I don't do as I'm told." He reached for Saul's neck and the horse nuzzled his fingers.

"Looks like you've made a friend, James." He

winked. "Must be all those apples you keep snea-kin' him."

"You knew about them apples?" The boy flushed and turned to run for home. "So long, Preacher."

Sarah stood on the porch shielding her eyes from the rising sun as she scanned the horizon for TJ. Right after breakfast, she'd harnessed Lightfoot and had her all ready to go. In her hand, TJ's usual biscuit, and on the porch rail, a cup of coffee with plenty of cream, the way he liked it.

There he was! Sun glinted from behind his back like a halo around his head. As he drew closer, his black hair shone like a raven's wings. Sarah couldn't take her eyes off of him. The way he sat on that horse liked to take her breath away. He rode right on past the well and straight to the porch, where she waited. And even though the sun was already heating up the air, she pulled her shawl closer, giving the impression of warm arms surrounding her.

He threw Saul's bridle over the porch rail and smiled at her, making her heart slam into her ribs. Could he hear it and know what she was thinking? She sucked back a deep breath and put her mind to the farm mat-ters. "Here you go. I figured you'd want to get started right away, so I brought your coffee and biscuit to the porch. Besides, the house is hot already with the stove going from the biscuits."

"Thank you kindly. I'll have a quick bite and go har-ness Lightfoot."

Sarah smiled and flushed to her embarrassment. Why was he affecting her this way? "She's all ready to start. I thought a break was in order. You deserve one.

And I'll take Saul in and rub him down, give him his oats." She placed the biscuits in a napkin next to his coffee and picked up Saul's bridle. When she did, she felt the half-shy expression that had taken over her face. TJ brought out the strangest feelings in her.

His nearness caused an odd mixture of joy and nervousness. The sun had nothing on the warmth he produced as she passed him and brushed against his shoulder. "Pardon me."

TJ turned with her, took her hand in his. "Thank you. You're always thinking of other folks before yourself. This'll taste right fine."

She stared at the ground. If she looked him in the eyes, she'd start crying for all the kindness he was showing her and Zach. She shivered with the truth. Maybe she didn't dare look him in the eye for other reasons—for fear he'd be able to tell how she was beginning to feel.

Wednesday came and went, Sarah cooking and doing the farm chores, and TJ plowing. Grateful for the fine meals and water breaks, he found himself actually enjoying the manual work. Felt closer to God, as well. Praying came easy with the smell of fresh-turned earth beneath his feet. The closer connection surprised him. The dirt's smell, the look of the neat, clean rows, the manure mixing with the earth, all filled his head and his heart in a way that riding town to town hadn't provided in the past. Surprised at this change of heart, he had to ask himself whether or not he would be comfortable staying in one town, preaching to one group of folks, finding a small plot of land and farming for himself.

He stopped Lightfoot and reached down, sifted the

rich dirt through his fingers, suddenly realizing why Nathaniel had brought Sarah to the Dakota Territory. Seeing tomatoes and beans growing must have lured him to the farm life. So different from TJ's plans.

Nowhere would a person find this type of solitude and prayerful existence in a city. Was Boston like New York? He supposed so. All big cities no doubt crammed their new inhabitants into rows and rows of small dwellings and then worked them nearly to death. With the recently arrived so grateful to be in their new country, he realized from experience that they would gladly live anywhere and do any job just to say they were Americans.

TJ sighed. That part of his life was done and over. His past. His present meant preaching, riding circuit for the four towns. He faithfully rode the circuit every four weeks. Soon Paceoff and Tideville wouldn't need a part-time preacher if Robert Jennings, a friend from back east, decided to come out. Robert could take over those two and leave Gullywash and Lost Cap to TJ. His heart stuttered. If that were the case, he'd be spending a lot more time in Gullywash. A mere breath away from Sarah and Zachary Rycroft.

After turning over the last row of the day, TJ headed for the barn to rub down Lightfoot and give her an extra measure of feed for all her hard work. As he pulled back the heavy door on the front of the barn, he couldn't help but notice the fine job Nathaniel had done with this structure as well as the house. Obviously one for details, he had taken great care that outside predators wouldn't be able to penetrate any areas of the barn. Well, of course, mice could, but Sarah had solved that issue with Sassy. Had Nathaniel perhaps been a carpenter before he left Boston? A rather large barn, it had three stalls for horses and plenty of room for the growing number of cows. The pigs had their own separate section, and, of course, the chickens their own coop, not attached to the main structure. A split-rail fence enclosed the entire area and made for a neat and clean dwelling for all the livestock.

Lightfoot nickered and nuzzled TJ's hand. "There you go, girl. Good day's work. You are a hard worker, little lady."

His head swam with ideas for improvements on the place when Sarah called, "Supper's on! Get washed up, you two."

If he stayed, he'd be drawn that much closer to the woman who had inadvertently captured his heart, and if he didn't stay, he would feel cheated somehow. And he wasn't thinking only about supper. His thoughts had drifted to staying closer to this farm for good.

He shouted over his shoulder, "Give me five minutes to tend to Lightfoot."

Was the pull here strong enough for him to have to rethink his vow to God?

Sarah would give him an hour if that was what he needed. Little by little each day, he had wriggled his way into her heart. What man did all of this plowing and tending if he didn't care? TJ was such an honorable man and put her life and Zach's above his own comfort. Preachers didn't do all that in order to pull another lost sheep into their flocks, did they?

She gazed around her kitchen, useful and bright and sunny. That had been the only luxury she had asked for in a house. She wanted to spend her time in a cheerful kitchen, and Nathaniel had obliged by putting in two big windows across the back of the house. That way when she looked out, she could watch Nathaniel working the land and Zach playing in the back. They had planned it all so beautifully. Only thing they hadn't planned on... Nathaniel's horse running under a low branch.

Two years. A lifetime ago, and she needed to move on. Every single thing inside her told her so. There was only one man she wanted to move on with, TJ O'Brien. A sigh racked her body. She turned quickly. Had anyone heard? Hopefully not. She must maintain a respectful distance. So why had she taken such care with her appearance today? And cooked like a crazy woman.

Tonight she'd made ham and potatoes baked in their skins. With a thick lump of butter drizzling into the potatoes' mealy goodness, she was sure he'd be pleased. And pieplant pie from her spring canning. She giggled, remembering Zach's first taste of pieplant. His face had wrinkled into a mass of creases as he tried to spit it out and still tell her how good it was. Always the thoughtful little man. The plants they'd brought with them had taken nearly four years to grow strong enough to use. Nathaniel hadn't lived long enough to taste it.

Well, now the preacher would. She'd serve him a big piece of the pie...if he liked pieplant. Maybe... Never mind. That was what was for supper. If he liked it, so be it. If not, too bad.

She dusted flour from her fingers and patted loose strands of hair into place. No need to look as if she'd been working all day, even though she had. She'd milked the cows, gathered eggs with Zach, fed the chickens, horses and cows, forked fresh straw onto their beds, cleaned out manure for the field, which she'd then hauled out bucket by bucket. All that before she'd started dinner, let alone supper. But after her chores, she'd spent a few minutes fussing, trying to look her best.

Exhausted just thinking about it, she called, "Zach, time to come in." Her voice carried out the back door to where he played with his kitten. Small, rapid steps skipped in the back while heavy footfalls crossed the front porch. A lump lodged in her throat, and she had to swallow twice to force it away.

She quickly finished setting the table. A slight knock and TJ entered, not waiting for her to invite him in. They had grown quite comfortable with each other in the past couple of days. "Fresh water in the pantry," she told him. "Go ahead and wash. I'll dish up supper."

"Thank you for thinking of it. I'll be a minute."

"Take your time." She smiled at his back. "Zach, you wash up, too. No dirty hands at the table."

As her son turned to follow TJ, Sarah pinched her cheeks to give them life. Too late. He rounded the corner and caught her with her fingers pinching at her face. They certainly were pink now.

He strode to her side and brushed at her hair. "You baked today?"

"How did you know? You smelled the pie?"

"No, and I do love pie. But you have flour in your hair."

"Where? I was so careful to—"

"You were, huh?" His chuckle caused her to nip the edge of her lip, embarrassed he'd caught the one bunch of hair in disarray. "You look sweet, Sarah. The way I would expect a wife to look in the evening."

Then it was his turn to flame red. He started to apologize, but the words didn't come out.

Sarah thought it best to begin dinner before both of them proved unequal to the task of speaking without rambling. "Zach, come along. Supper's on."

"Aww, Mama. Sassy wanted her milk."

"Zachary Rycroft."

"Yes, ma'am." His little feet rushed across the floor and he held his hands out to her. "See, Mama. All clean. Lookit. I even washed my face."

She kissed his fingers and lifted him into his chair.

TJ grabbed their hands and bowed his head. "Lord, we thank You for this fine meal that Sarah prepared. Bless her for seeing to our needs with care. Bless the food to our bodies in the name of Your Son, Jesus. Amen."

Sarah opened her eyes to a gentle smile curling the edges of his lips. She needed to say something or die of embarrassment that he'd caught her primping for him. "Can you use one of the roans for plowing in the morning? I'd like to go into town, and Lightfoot's a tad easier on the bit with me."

He set down his cup and leaned toward Sarah. "Do you want me to drive you?"

"No. I'll be fine." Her head listed to the side. "Thought Zach might like to take the extra pie I baked to the Redfords. They've been so kind to us."

TJ stopped eating, and Sarah had to wonder what he was thinking. That look he gave her…as if questioning her true motives for the trip to town. He didn't know. He couldn't. So why the gaze that left her feeling exposed to the world?

"Soon that first field is going to be finished." His

eyes bored into her. "I have no doubt you'll get a good crop, Sarah. If you're worried about that, you needn't be."

Putting her mind at ease had become a favorite pastime for the preacher. For TJ. And Sarah decided in her heart that their friendship seemed to have passed the point of preacher and widow. "No. I'm not worried... much." She laughed. "I guess it's my nature to worry. You've seen Zach when he gets going. You'd worry, too, if you had to chase him around all day." In truth, she worried over everything. Zach, the farm, the fields and more. Since she was a child, she'd been a worrier, a fact her mother had pointed out far too many times. But a man who'd had an easy life, even if he was a man of God, couldn't understand that, now, could he?

Chapter 13

"But I've made up my mind, Molly." Sarah stomped her foot much the same way she'd seen Zach do when he wasn't getting his own way, and her face instantly burned with shame. She sat back down and drew strength from Molly's good strong chamomile tea with lemon before addressing her behavior. She sipped the calming drink, avoiding Molly's questioning gaze.

"I'm sorry. I feel like Zach when he throws a fit. It's just that there isn't anything else I can do. I figure Margaret Baker's son David will buy them from me. I've heard that when he goes to the city he sells items he's acquired from folks."

Molly shook her head, her face like stone as she filled their cups once again. "Yes, I believe his mother told the sheriff that very thing when a necklace came up missing a year ago. David Baker didn't steal it, but he knew all about the piece and was able to help find out where it had been sold." She sat down in her seat and peered over the top of her spectacles. "Sarah, your trying to save that farm is admirable, but at some point you will have to stop fighting. There won't be anything left. Now, I want you and Zachary to stay in Gullywash so much that my husband and I have discussed what we might do to help, but the truth is, we don't have any money socked away in a drawer. If we did, it would be yours."

"Oh, no."

"Listen to what I have to say. Don't interrupt."

"Sorry." She couldn't let them. Not even if they had scads of money lying about.

"We love you and the boy like you were our own. That little fella brings us so much joy. And you are a dear girl who deserves better than what life's thrown at you. But that's all part of living…and dying. We don't know what the next day will bring. And that is my point here. You might sell that ring and watch, and if it's not enough for that mean old snake at the bank, then you'll be without your prized possessions and no closer to saving your farm. Do you see what I'm trying to tell you, dear? Is that really what you want?"

Sarah's mind wandered and she didn't seem to be able to pull it back into the conversation. Molly was right about one thing: Studdard might not give her more time if it wasn't the full amount. But she had to try. "It's not like I'll lose my pa and Nathaniel when I sell the ring and the watch, because they're tucked right here—" she tapped her chest "—in my heart. That's what truly matters. And Nathaniel would never forgive me for letting the farm go over a piece of gold.

I believe he'd want me to sell this ring." Sarah rolled it around her finger until tears filled the backs of her eyes. "I have to do it, Molly. I just have to. Nathaniel worked hard to build that farm into what it is today, and I can't let him down."

"Lands, Sarah. You have to do what you think's right. Here." Molly pulled a muslin napkin from a drawer in the sideboard and handed it to her.

She dabbed her tears away.

"You are a smart girl, and if you think this could save your property, then you go see David Baker and strike a bargain. Make a sound deal, a fair deal with him, and I'll be praying that one way or the other the good Lord honors it for you."

"What would I do without you, Molly?" She rose and kissed her friend's cheek. "Like my own mother."

"Oh, go on with you."

Not waiting another second where she might change her mind, Sarah folded the napkin and placed it back on the table. Her fingers fluttered over the cup until she took one last sip of tea for courage and attempted another smile at Molly. Standing, hands on her hips, she said, "Well, there's no time like the present. I hear David is set to leave in another week. A trip to Minneapolis, I think Mrs. Baker said. So I'd best get a move on. You sure you don't mind Zach staying? You've seen to him quite a few times this past month."

"You'd better stop asking that." Molly grinned. "Can't get enough of the sweet child. Besides, the man and me'll love this pieplant pie. I'm not even going to wait for him to get home."

Sarah wished she could wait. Wait forever before selling the beloved heirlooms.

* * *

TJ drew Zach onto his lap. "She been cryin' long, son?"

"We said goodbye to Aunt Molly and Mama cried. We gots in the wagon and she cried. We gots home, and she cried."

He smoothed hair back from the boy's forehead. "Don't worry about her, Zach. Even grown-ups have days that are hard for them."

"They do? You sure?"

"They do. And when folks we love are having a difficult time, we pray for them. Would you like to pray with me before I fix dinner?"

Zach's face scrunched into a half frown, half smile. "Boys can cook?"

"When I'm on the road, I cook for myself a lot. Are you surprised?"

"I surprised." He grinned. "Whatcha gonna make?"

He set Zach on the floor and pointed to the kitchen. "Why don't you come help me?"

"May I?"

"You surely may. I'll let you show me where the bread is and we'll make some butter-and-honey sandwiches."

"Yum. My favorite."

TJ laughed. "I think you have a lot of favorites, young man."

Zach giggled all the way into the kitchen and then stopped abruptly. "Will we wake up Mama?"

"I doubt she's asleep, but we'll be quiet in case, all right?"

Zach nodded, so serious and grown-up that TJ could almost imagine what a serious moment with Nathaniel would have looked like. Of course, he didn't know for certain, but with all he'd heard about Nathaniel, he believed they could have been good friends.

"Zach?"

They both turned at the sound of Sarah's voice.

"I'll be right out to fix dinner."

TJ held a finger to his lips and walked toward the back room. "Sarah, you decent?"

"I should hope so."

"Just wanna poke my head in." He inched the door open. "I'm fixing some bread and milk for the two of us, so why don't you rest a bit. I'm going to take Zach out to the field with me while I finish for the day." Before she could put into words what her frown already saying, TJ whispered, "I don't mind. Let me help you. And I'd like to show him all I've done to the fields so we'll have a good crop next spring."

And with that, she burst out crying again and he closed the door, unsure what he'd said to upset her.

Her ringless finger dared her to forget what she'd done. Sarah hadn't thought it would hurt this much... her wedding band gone, as if the last piece of her life with Nathaniel had been ripped away. But it was her choice. So why was the pain so strong? Because it had probably all been for nothing. Her trip to the bank had been a disaster.

She replayed the entire scene in her mind.

Why, Mrs. Rycroft. How lovely to see you.

I hope you'll feel the same once I've talked to you, Mr. Studdard.

He pulled back the chair in front of his desk—the chair that had begun to feel like a jail cell to Sarah.

Have a seat. He sat on the corner of his desk, his head above hers, seeming twice as intimidating. *Now, what can I help you with?*

I brought money. The words were quick and to the point. She had to say it before she changed her mind.

You what?

I have...part of the money for the note. She dug into the small brocade reticule in her lap and pulled out the paper money. *I can pay you part now and part in the spring.*

Mrs. Rycroft—

Please, Mr. Studdard. It's all I have in the world.

He accepted the bills and put them into the drawer in his desk. *I will do this, though I know it's not at all what I should be doing for the bank. I will give you one more week.*

She jumped from her seat. *One week?* Her hand over her chest, the tears began their too-familiar sting. *I can't get any more money in a week.*

Well, that's the best I can do. Next Thursday I'll expect to see you in here by ten o'clock or we will consider you didn't make good on the note. That's all, Mrs. Rycroft. One more week. Do you understand?

Sarah turned away from him only to see the look of pity on Myra Brekenridge's face.

Without one more glance in his direction, Sarah dragged her feet, heavier than saddles around her ankles, outside into the bright sun.

As if to insult Sarah further, he shouted after her, *No later than ten o'clock next Thursday, Mrs. Rycroft.*

One week and for what? She had nothing left to sell unless folks hereabouts would forget his stories about the livestock. She walked past Haleys' and reached her hand out for an apple from the large bin in the front. She wrapped her fingers around it and threw the thing as far as she could, smashing it against a watering trough. Then she spun around to see Mrs. Haley standing hands on hips, watching her.

"You all right, girl?"

"Forgive me. I, uh… I'm so sorry, Mrs. Haley. Here—" she dug into the small bag a second time "—let me pay you."

Mrs. Haley held up her hand and tried to force a smile to her lips. "Go on with you." Then she did the strangest thing. She pulled alongside Sarah and murmured, "I'm not one for gossip, Mrs. Rycroft, but I did hear tell that the banker is giving you trouble because he wants your property. Child, if I had the wherewithal to buy those animals of yours, I would, but with everyone losing most of their crops, I'm having to extend too much credit as it is. I'm real sorry, Mrs. Rycroft. You've been good to me. Wish I could return the favor. But the apple, well, it's my treat for the day if you'll make me a promise."

Sarah sniffled. "What would that be?"

"Next time, you put that apple right between his eyes…for both of us."

That image sent Sarah into a fit of giggles. "I promise."

TJ saw no purpose in trying to plow with Zach next to him. Too dangerous for the boy, so he let Zach ride Lightfoot back to the barn and then sit on his shoulders while he rubbed her down and gave her water. "Hang on tight, young man."

"I will." Laughter accompanied each task and TJ wondered what it would be like to have a son of his own. Zachary Rycroft was the sweetest little boy he'd ever been around. Were they all like Zach? No, probably not. He was sweet because he'd learned about life from his mother. And she was one sweet woman.

Stop that. No sense crying over what you can't have.

Once they'd finished chores and headed toward the house, TJ ruffled the hair on Zach's head the same way he ran his fingers through his own. "Zachary, do you take a nap in the afternoon?"

"Sometimes."

His best stern look took over. "Zach?"

"Yes, sir. I takes a nap."

"Okay, let's go in, have one of those cookies Mrs. Redford sent back with a glass of milk and then you take a nap. Just a short one. All right? Because you really are growing too big to be taking long naps. Wouldn't you say so?"

Zach kicked at the clump of rough rye grass under his foot. "All right."

After the boy went down for a nap, TJ started his search of the panty. Eggs, a slab of pork in a brine crock, fresh bread. And he knew the garden was ripe with tomatoes and beans. Plenty to fix a supper for all of them.

First he mixed up a batch of biscuit dough, the same kind his uncle used to make. Plenty of saleratus so they'd rise fat and fall apart in the mouth. Then he set it aside while he walked out to the garden. A bounty of vegetables grew on vines and along the ground. The pumpkins were tinting with orange and he could almost taste pumpkin pie. Sarah, a fine cook in her own right, would make some man… He groaned. He didn't want her making some man a good wife. He wanted

Sarah. Wanted her so badly for himself that he ached to his bones.

No sense dwelling on it; there was supper to fix. Tomatoes, beans and three ears of corn. He could cook every bit as well as Mrs. Loiller, and he would. Sarah had taken wonderful care of him while he worked the field. He could take care of her for a change.

Hot coffee bubbled on the stove as he grabbed a cloth and doubled it to pull out the biscuits. Once he finished stirring the pork gravy, he called over his shoulder, "Supper's ready! Zach. Sarah. Wash up and come to the table."

The last thing he needed was milk for Zach. He dashed down to the cellar and brought up the pitcher Sarah kept full for meals. He poured a glass for the boy and set the pitcher on the table next to the small dish of honey for the biscuits.

Sarah's face, red from crying, appeared with a look of surprise. "You did this?"

Zach clapped and jumped around the table until Sarah had to say, "Zach, that will be enough."

"Sorry, Mama. But Mis-ter O'Brien said boys can cook. And he did." The boy took his seat and TJ winked over Sarah's head.

"I've been known to cook right well." He chuckled. "My uncle taught me how."

"Your uncle?"

He waited for her to sit and then took his seat. "Yes, we lived in a…rather poor area in New York City. My uncle thought it was his job to take in all the immigrants coming from Ireland who had nowhere else to go. And my uncle was not a rich man."

"I thought—"

"Doesn't matter. We were happy as twelve folks can be in one very crowded tenement in the middle of the city. We got by. When my folks died, they had $200 they'd put aside for me for schooling. And my uncle refused to touch it. Said the money would give me a start one day. Then when scarlet fever hit, the children died, all but two. And I prayed for their safety. That was the night I promised the Lord I'd become a preacher."

"You promised God..."

"And here I am. None the worse for wear, and my uncle still helps folks coming into the country. Says it's the least he can do for being blessed. A couple years after I made my vow he sent me off...with the money... and with his blessing."

"I had no idea. I thought since you came from the city... Well, never you mind what I thought."

"I see." So she thought he came from money. Where did she get that idea?

"I'm sorry. Most of the folks I knew in Boston were wealthy. I'll be honest with you. I didn't know a lot of poor families. Actually, I didn't know any."

TJ loaded Zach's plate. Poured gravy over one of the biscuits, spread honey on the other. Then he served a heaping spoonful of beans and bright yellow corn he'd cut from the ears. A dish of tomatoes with cream and sugar filled the small dishes next to their plates.

"Ooh, Mama. Look. My favorite."

Both TJ and Sarah laughed. So good to see her smile.

"Zach, would you like to pray over the meal?"

Chapter 14

Zach praying? The sweet man had taught her boy to pray. *Lord, I'm still trusting You, whatever You decide for our lives. It hurt today, no doubt about that, but if You want us to stay, no banker will stop us, and if You want us to go, then I won't try and stop us. It's all in Your hands.*

Sarah draped Zach's napkin over his shirtfront. "You and Mr. O'Brien had a busy day today?"

Zach giggled and tried to talk with his mouth full. "We was—"

TJ patted the back of Zach's hand. "Zach. Don't talk with food in your mouth."

"Sorry, sir."

"You know, your mama's taught you right fine manners. But how about if you call me Mr. TJ?" He looked to Sarah for approval and she nodded. "For now."

What did he mean by that? For now. Well, of course, if they stayed in town, as Zach grew up, he'd have to start calling him Mr. O'Brien again or TJ or Preacher once he was an adult. That was all he'd meant. "That's nice isn't it, Zach? Yes, you may call him Mr. TJ if you like." She stared at her plate. "I'm still amazed at this meal. It might have been one my own mother cooked. Thank you, TJ. Seems I needed that rest after all."

He gave a lopsided grin. "Thought you might." Then he proceeded to act distracted and ill at ease through the remainder of supper. He wouldn't look at her and barely talked.

"You have something on your mind?" she asked. "You seem… I don't know." She smiled. "Well, to have something on your mind."

He stood and started to clear the dishes.

"No need for that. You cooked. I'll clean up."

"I thought after Zach was put down for the night, we might have a talk."

"All right." A talk about what? The plowing. He shouldn't do any more plowing now that the farm was being lost to the banker. Unless she could come up with some way… No. She'd done all she could short of a miracle, and miracles didn't happen today. They might have once upon a time when Jesus and His disciples actually walked the earth, but not now. And even if they did, not for her.

Before Sarah would clear the dishes and make Zach ready for bed, she offered TJ more coffee. He accepted it and strolled out on the porch, where he sat on the steps. Through the doorway she saw him hunched over his cup with his long legs jutting out in front. Was he thinking of her or how fast he could skedaddle out of town and away from her problems? She would have to tell him what had happened in town today.

The faint sound of singing caused shivers to run along TJ's spine. Sarah's voice. No longer crying, she sang sweetly as she put her son to sleep. From tears of sorrow to pure joy all in one afternoon. Well, that was women for you. Right about the time when he thought he might have an inkling, she up and changed. He snapped his fingers. Just like that.

She had been feeling mighty good one day and weepy the next. Was that how women always behaved? He shook his head. Drawing the fresh coffee to his lips, he sipped too quickly and nearly burned his mouth, so he set the cup down to cool. He licked the side of his lip, offering a bit of comfort to the tender skin.

Then he leaned on his elbow and took in the land as dusk settled like a purple veil. Fireflies had started to flit about. First a handful here and there, and then there were dozens. Had Zach ever begged his mother for a canning jar to catch them in? Or had the little fellow's life been mostly hard work, as much as a boy his age could handle? TJ wondered as he pondered how productive this farm could be...with the right hands tending it. Then Zach could grow up enjoying childhood some.

Would God allow him to have it all? To preach, to tend a farm, to be a husband and father? And if God allowed it, would Sarah even want him? A beautiful woman like Sarah Rycroft deserved more than a cowboy preacher. She should have a wealthy suitor so she could tend only the house, only her boy. Besides that, she didn't believe anymore, and how could he be a preacher with a wife who didn't believe? *A wife.*

He scratched his head and slapped his palm against the porch boards, nearly upending his cup. So many questions and no answers. No, he had to remember his solemn oath. To live for God. Sarah would lose this farm and go back east. And there was nothing he could do to help. He needed to stop mulling over possibilities that could never happen.

When he looked up from his list of complaints, he saw hundreds of tiny creatures lighting the area past the porch and beyond. It took his breath away for a moment. Then he marveled at the beauty all around him. This farm was more than a livelihood for Sarah and Zach; it was her lifeblood. She had come here practically a child bride with her child husband, and they had proven themselves worthy, and Sarah continued to prove herself.

Light footsteps neared the door. TJ rose and took Sarah's elbow as she came out of the house. They sat on the porch, side by side, not saying much, merely watching the spectacular light show in front of them. Soon his hands began to sweat. Her breath blew across his cheek soft and warm when she faced him. "Nice evening. Pretty with the fireflies and all."

"Zach in bed?" What an ignorant question. Of course he was in bed. That was why she had washed him up and sung to him. The only reason she'd be out here. "I meant...do you have some free time now?"

"TJ, we do need to talk, like you said."

"What had you all riled today?"

"Riled? You're right there. I *was* riled." Her fingers twisted in her lap. Then she stood and leaned against the porch rail. "I went to see Banker Studdard. I came up with fifty dollars and asked him to give me more time."

He gazed up at her and finally rose to stand alongside her, his back pressing into the wood porch frame. Her eyes sparkled with the light of the moon, or was it tears? "Where did you come up with fifty dollars? I didn't think you sold any of the livestock, Sarah." Maybe there had been money left by her husband for just such an urgent situation, but she would have told him that. He was sure.

She turned to face him. "I didn't sell any of the livestock. Oh, TJ, I sold my ring and my pa's gold pocket watch."

"You what?" He grabbed her shoulders. "Your ring?"

"Now, don't *you* get riled." She put her hand over his and sighed. "I had to try, TJ. I just had to. I guess I didn't realize how little value they both had."

"What did that sorry excuse for a man, Studdard, give you for them?"

"I didn't sell them to Mr. Studdard." She looked away, but he drew her back to face him.

"Then who?"

"There's a man in town who buys and sells. He was kind enough to give me top dollar for them. But top dollar wasn't enough to convince the banker to give me more time."

"What did Studdard say to you?"

"He said no. And while it bothered me something fierce, I'm all right about it. God is in control of my life, not me."

"What happened to that lady who didn't want God in her affairs anymore?" Again her eyes held that twinkle he hadn't seen before. And she was smiling… openly.

"Oh, she grew up along the way. Made amends with God. Decided being in control wasn't as important as giving up the reins. I had to learn to trust, TJ."

Trust.

"My life was getting worse by the day—no, by the minute—and I had to let go."

Her words, like rain, fell on his heart, cleansing the doubts. Was this God's way of telling him it was all right? Did he dare ask her the most important question in the world? Did he even want to? She stood in front of him with her face tilted up, questioning his next words. If he bent ever so slightly, their mouths would touch.

He jerked back. No, sir. Not on your life. He didn't know how to kiss a woman and little Zach in there was proof she'd been kissed before—and kissed good.

He turned and scrubbed at his hair again. But as sure as the sun would rise, he wanted to kiss her. Could he trust himself to do it right, or would he make a worse fool of himself?

A gentle touch on his arm spun him around. "Are you all right?"

Those beautiful lips and her sweet face. Here she was worrying about saving her farm, and she wanted to know if he was all right. He licked his lips to speak, and she stood on her toes, closed her eyes and invited the kiss he longed to give her.

Without another care to all of his endless thoughts and worries, he leaned toward her. Her breath, sweet like honey, reached out to him.

"Mama! Mama! Come quick."

Sarah dropped from her toes and spun for the door, TJ right behind her.

* * *

What a time for Zach to call her name. Only a nightmare. Sarah eased out a long sigh and looked at TJ, his face a mishmash of worry. "It's all right. He has bad dreams now and then. You should run along home. Give Molly and her husband my best."

"If you're certain he's all right."

With little else to say, she nodded. "He's fine. Every now and then he dreams someone's out to snatch him. I have no idea where the thought comes from, but when he has them, I take him into bed with me. Thank you for cooking such a fine supper for us." She couldn't stop her gaze from following the line of his square jaw, his midnight expression. He had nearly kissed her, she was sure. But now... Well, more important things to deal with than a kiss. Besides, it had been so long she might have forgotten how to kiss a man. "Good night, Preacher." She felt the blush. "I mean, TJ. Can you see yourself out?"

"Yes, ma'am." He tipped a small salute in her direction and shifted on his heel. "Well, good night, then." As he opened the door wide, he offered another wave. "I'll be going."

Pulling the bed quilt tighter around Zach's shoulders, Sarah noticed that he'd stopped whimpering. When she walked into the front room, she remembered the coffee cup left on the porch. Might as well take care of it tonight as wait till morning. An animal might come along and break it. And no way would she take a chance on losing a piece of her china.

She pulled her shawl back over her shoulders and headed out front. Darkness had wholly set in. All but the fireflies and night sounds that carried across the land. Crickets made their mating calls and the fireflies seemed to dance to the rhythmic sounds. Her land was more than beautiful, but it was also now in God's hands. As she closed the door behind her, she nearly missed TJ sitting on the steps, only a faint silhouette. "Is anything wrong?" she asked.

The dark figure turned. He removed his hat and set it on the porch. Then he stood. In spite of the darkness, his eyes shone like Zach's marbles. And his gaze pierced to her core.

"Wh-why are you still out here?"

A heavy groan exploded from his chest. "Oh, Sarah!" His feet covered the porch in two steps. Then he crushed her to him and leveled a gaze that said, "No more talk." His lips brushed hers gently, then he stopped. Froze.

TJ hadn't expected to kiss her. He stared into her eyes. He didn't know what he was doing. Maybe merely making a fool of himself. Never having kissed a woman before, he might be making a complete mess of things. As his heart thudded in his ears, he pressed his forehead against hers, trying not to shake. "Sarah," he murmured. "I'm afraid—"

She put soft fingers over his mouth. He pressed forward and kissed them, all the time speaking her name over and over. When she didn't pull away, he wrapped her in his arms so completely he couldn't tell where he stopped and she started, as if the good Lord had created them to be a perfect fit. "Oh, Sarah." His lips couldn't wait another second. And this time, there was nothing hesitant and gentle about the way his mouth sought hers. Warm and welcoming, she kissed him back until his heart and soul took over for his lack of experience. Her lips were sweeter than honey, as he thought they would be, so much so that he couldn't bring himself to part from her.

"Whoa." She stepped back, breaking his hold. "As much as I don't want to, I think we'd better say goodnight."

Her warmth slipped away with her, leaving his arms empty and cold, his lips fighting not to lose the sweet taste she left behind. *Don't stop now. Not when we've finally kissed. Come back, Sarah.* A groan ran from his belly to his lips, but he stopped it just in time. "Are you sure?"

"Perhaps you should ride on out." Her words said one thing, but that look in her eyes said another. Wasn't that look asking him to stay? Maybe a few minutes longer? No, he had to leave now or there would be talk.

Steadying himself as he leaned down and picked up his hat along with the cup, he questioned his actions one more time. "I do believe you're right, ma'am. Now's as good a time as any." He handed her the cup, but the minute their hands touched, he wanted to forget all good intentions and hold her to him once more, feel her soft mouth against his lips. From the longing in her expression, she felt the same.

And he'd thought life as a child could be complicated. His life here and now was driving him crazy. Sarah had given him all sorts of reasons to change the life he'd grown to love. His aloneness had become just that, alone. And he didn't like it anymore. Yet her reputation in town would be ruined if he didn't leave, and right this second. "Yes, well, good night, then."

One thing was for certain and for sure: he had to figure out a way for her to keep the farm and for him to let God know he planned to honor his promise but with a wife at his side.

Sarah remained on the porch as TJ trudged to the barn. When he rode out, she waved her hand but doubted he could see her through the darkness. Did he sense her presence? Maybe, maybe not. Funny how he'd been unsure of her at first. Her face burned to think of the way she'd kissed him back, as her mother would say, "like a floozy." But he hadn't seemed to mind even though he was a preacher. Did she mind? Not at all. When he kissed her, Nathaniel's face hadn't clouded her feelings, not for a second, and she knew that while she'd always love him, always have room for him in her heart, she now had room for another, as well.

She put fingers to lips that still tingled from his touch. Had he kissed her like that because he cared about her, wanted to be with her, or simply because she was there? A woman. Whatever the reason, her knees had grown weak and her insides had fluttered like a frightened bird.

Two years.

It had been two years since she'd been kissed by a man. And how she'd missed the closeness, the comfort. Sarah's feet shuffled to the door, the weight of uncertainty heavy in her heart. From the first day TJ had ridden onto her property, his attractiveness had awakened feelings deep inside that she had thought dead and buried. When he had caught Zach, his protective nature toward him had awakened it, and his attentiveness to her had forced the feelings to life.

Her head screamed that she was betraying Nathaniel, but her heart told her she was beginning to live again. She suddenly realized she didn't have to ask herself which way she would follow. Her steps had walked in TJ's direction the minute his lips had taken hers.

Chapter 15

TJ shook his head at the sheriff. "I don't see any other choice in the matter."

Redford nodded. "No, I don't guess there is another way. If your mind's set on it, do it right quick. No time like the present. Otherwise you might decide different."

Still rubbing sleep from his eyes after a troubled night tossing and turning in bed, TJ swallowed the last bite of his biscuit. "If only there were another way, believe me, I'd take it, but that banker has her over a barrel. It's going to be embarrassing to see him sitting in his seat at services knowing what I know about the man."

"I'll be honest—if I had a way I could bring him in and hold him till she found a way to pay, I'd do it. His pa was one of the founders of Gullywash. He was honest, hardworking and would have a hard time with the direction his boy has taken. If I thought the town could help out, I'd go door to door, but I know only a handful of folks who didn't lose their shirts this month."

"Sad all round," TJ added.

"Here," the sheriff offered, "have another biscuit before you go. Molly said to finish these from last night's supper. They won't taste near so good by dinnertime." He pushed the platter closer. "I made the right call, you know."

"About?"

"About you. You're more than just a preacher—you're a good man, Terrance. A fine man who will make a first-rate addition to this community if you ever have a mind to settle in one place."

Accepting the platter, TJ slid another of the flaky biscuits onto his plate. Then he slathered the insides with butter and Molly's berry jam. "This is delicious. Molly's a wonderful cook."

"She's a good wife in every way. A very good wife. What you need about now."

"Oh, don't you start, too. Molly was as bad as that Loiller woman the other day. Did everything but show me some of Sarah's knitting and whatnot. You be glad you're married. Being single and on the road is like putting a noose around your neck." A noose that had begun to look better and better.

Redford licked a speck of jam from his thumb. "I know what I'm talkin' about, boy. Men shy away from marriage like a horse from a cliff, but a good upstanding Christian woman is as a scarce as snakes' legs. When you find one, you should hang on to her with both hands." He winked. "Surefire pleasant way to go through life. Both hands around a beautiful woman."

"You might be right there, too."

The sheriff's brows waggled up his forehead. "Well, now. So it isn't merely a just cause you've undertaken. You want to impress the widow Rycroft. Not bad."

"I'd have to do a heap more than this to impress her. I don't think deep down she cottons to me much. Maybe as a friend or worker. I can assure you, that's all." But he choked at the red creeping over his face remembering last night's kiss. His first kiss ever. What a fumbling mess he'd made of that until she'd kissed him back and taught him a thing or two. And he couldn't very well ask the sheriff about kissing, now, could he? Heat crept down his collar as well and, flustered, he jammed in another mouthful of biscuit.

He looked up at the studying expression on the sheriff's face. Was he reading his mind? Could he tell what'd happened between them?

"You think that's all, eh? I can tell you, boy, you aren't the smartest student in the class."

TJ tugged at his collar so he could swallow without the food sticking. His muscles were so tight he thought he might pop if he didn't leave soon. The sheriff didn't act coy like Molly; he said what he had to say outright, and TJ had grown downright uncomfortable.

He rose from his chair, leaving the second biscuit half-eaten on his plate. "Tell Molly thank you very much for the fine breakfast. Can't eat another bite. But it was mighty good. Yesirree, mighty good indeed." *Stop going on so. He can't tell you kissed Sarah last night. No way does he know.* Only he and Sarah knew. And that was enough.

Sheriff Redford grinned an irritating smirk that said he was somehow superior to the kid in front of him.

Well, TJ might be younger, less experienced than Sheriff Redford, but he was no kid. And he'd make up his own mind about such matters.

Steering the conversation away from his problems, he said, "Don't forget to tell your wife I'm much obliged."

Supporting his weight on the edge of the table, the sheriff chuckled as he blew out a breath. "I'll tell 'er. You run along and get done what you have to. Will we be seein' you for dinner?"

"I plan to finish the plowing if I ever get started."

With an irritating wave and cluck of his cheek, the sheriff sent him on his way.

Without his saddle, Saul clopped from the barn looking naked in TJ's eyes. Could he do this for real? He patted Saul's neck and stroked his long ears. His voice, barely above a whisper, murmured, "I'll miss you, fella. I might see you from time to time, but I'll miss you just the same. You've been a true and faithful servant, boy."

"Hey, Preacher. How's that horse o' yours?" James Studdard ran to meet them at the edge of the sheriff's property.

"Just who I was looking for."

The boy's face lit up as he handed Saul an apple. "For me? What did you want with me?"

"I heard you've been saving for a fine animal like Saul. What say you and I cut a deal on him?"

Face suddenly pale, James stumbled over his words. "You'd...sell your horse? To me?"

"He won't come cheap. He's broke for riding. He's also harness broke, but I wouldn't do that to him if you want to keep him for yourself. He doesn't take to it much at all."

"No, sir. I wouldn't put him in harness, not for anything. He's as fine a horse as I've ever seen."

"You're a good judge, James. And I can tell you truly love him. I wouldn't be able to sell him to anyone else. Two hundred and twenty-five dollars and he's yours."

"Two hundred and twenty-five dollars? I'm sorry, Mr. O'Brien. I've saved only 200. And Pa said he'd take me to auction. I have to admit, though. I couldn't find a better animal at any auction. And I know how you've cared for him. It's obvious." James rubbed his chin, his tongue sticking out the edge, showing he was deep in thought.

TJ stroked Saul's neck again, then saw how he pulled to James's side. But if he got only 200, he'd have just fifty dollars to his name, barely enough to buy an old nag to get around. He had to stick to his obligations on the circuit, so he had to have a horse. Could he find one for fifty dollars?

"All right, James." He shoved his hand at the boy. "Two hundred dollars it is. Today. Right now. Your pa won't mind?"

"It's my money, and I know folks think he runs my life, but when it comes to horse flesh, my pa trusts me." James nearly fell over as he took off for home, stumbling across the gravel. "Be right back. Gotta go flip my mattress!"

"Bring back a bridle!" TJ shouted.

His mattress? He kept his money under his mattress, not even in his father's bank. Well, he knew his father better than most. Smart boy.

While James ran home, TJ walked inside the sheriff's house, where he wrote out a bill of sale for Saul. He hadn't done anything this difficult since the day he walked away from his uncle's.

"But you can't pay the widow's note!" Studdard almost growled out the words like a mangy cur.

"I most certainly can and I am."

"It isn't your mortgage!"

"Money's money, Mr. Studdard. Here you go."

But before Studdard could accept the $200, Myra Brekenridge stood and approached them. "That will be just $150." She looked at the banker, whose face was now redder than a ripe cherry. "I think it must have slipped your mind...her fifty dollars to hold the note another week. Isn't that right, Mr. Studdard...sir?"

"Of course. One hundred and fifty. I almost forgot she paid fifty in good faith." He narrowed a gaze at Mrs. Brekenridge that told TJ she would pay dearly for her outburst.

TJ didn't budge, nor did Mrs. Brekenridge, and TJ had to wonder who would pay the most. The expression and stance of Mrs. Brekenridge led him to believe Studdard would receive a dressing-down from his own employee. One he wouldn't soon forget.

With his eyes bulging and his breathing at a gallop, the banker grabbed the money and stuffed it into his desk. "Was there something else you wanted?" He spit out the words so angrily TJ dodged the moisture.

"Yes, sir, the signed note."

Studdard frowned. "What?"

Mrs. Brekenridge crossed her arms, her foot tapping out a beat on the floor. "The note, Mr. Studdard.

Marked paid. For Mrs. Rycroft. You need to hand it over to Mr. O'Brien."

Studdard licked his lips and turned away. "Of course, Myra! Take care of it. I'm going home for the rest of the day."

TJ smiled. And if Studdard wasn't ill enough, he'd be even worse when he saw TJ's bay in his stall. Putting two and two together, as good bankers do, he'd understand in a second where the money had come from. Poor James.

He hoped his grin was sufficient for Myra, but a kiss would only be better. After she finished with his papers, he dropped a peck on her cheek and then plopped his hat on his head. "Thank you, ma'am. I'm right proud to know you."

She pinked up rosier than a lady apple.

Then, even though Studdard had left, he leaned in and whispered, "You won't have trouble with him, will you?"

"Me? Trouble with him? I should say not. I know how to handle Mr. Studdard when times come that I have to. Don't you worry."

"You're a peach, ma'am."

"You tell Mrs. Rycroft I send my best to her. She knows I was hoping she'd keep her place. I'd be beholden to you."

TJ tipped his hat. "My pleasure."

Late morning and still no sign of TJ O'Brien. Well, she couldn't expect he'd spend every moment helping get her farm ready for planting. And after how forward she'd been last night, he might not ever show up here again. She probably scared him away a mile wide and ten miles deep.

She shooed Zach out the door after he convinced her he was still hungry. Two cookies and a glass of milk later, he was ready to head for the barn, where he and Sassy would hunt for mice. She giggled at the way he had taken to the kitty. Both of them too small for such antics, still they had managed to catch three mice since Sassy had come to live with them.

As they disappeared around the corner of the barn, she thought she saw someone walking from the direction of town. Now, who could that be? Maybe James had changed his mind and planned to help her with the plowing after all. Good. This was too much work for a woman to handle, and since it didn't seem TJ would be returning, she could use another set of hands.

She fled back into the house; help or no help, she had laundry to hang out. Besides, if that wasn't James, she wanted to be closer to her husband's rifle. Just in case.

TJ tipped his hat over his face against the bright sun, but as he drew closer to the farmhouse, he looked up in time to see the familiar barrel of Sarah's rifle. "Hey there. Not very friendly today, are you?"

"TJ? That you?"

"In the flesh. I'd like to keep that flesh without holes in it, if you don't mind putting that Winchester away."

She lowered the rifle and stepped out onto the porch. "It's so late. I didn't think you were coming. No more biscuits, but I've got cookies and there's still warm coffee left over on the stove."

"I had things to take care of in town. But I would much appreciate the coffee and I've been known to eat a cookie or two, as you well know." If he had his way, he'd share every meal from now on with Sarah. If she said yes. He fingered the paper in his pocket and the small packet next to it. Maybe this wasn't a good time to bring up how he felt about her; he didn't merely want her gratitude. Without a single doubt, he would have to be sure she cared for him. Even if it meant she would learn to love him in time. Right now he loved her enough for the both of them.

This beautiful morning caused him to want to burst out singing, but she'd think he was crazier than ever and that wouldn't help his cause.

"Come on in out of the sun, then. I'll pour the coffee."

When he removed his hat, she noticed how his face wrinkled in concern. No doubt worrying about her losing the farm. They'd become friends—more if she had her way, but friends nonetheless—and she was grateful for all he'd done to help.

"Would you like to sit a spell?" She indicated the chair and coffee she'd poured for him.

"That would be nice. I don't have much left in the field anyway. If Lightfoot's feeling well rested, we should be able to finish by afternoon."

Her gaze turned to the front door. "Lightfoot, of course." She hadn't seen his Saul. He walked here? "Did Saul throw a shoe? You walked all the way from town?"

He didn't look up but kept his head over his cup. "Beautiful day out today. Thought I'd stretch my legs a bit. Does a man poorly if he rides all the time. He gets fat and lazy."

"That was quite a stretch you gave your legs. Better than two miles in this heat."

"Yes, ma'am. Sometimes a fella's gotta use his legs. All this riding isn't healthy."

She sat in the chair next to his. "TJ, what's going on? I've never known you to be so quiet, for one. And then Saul's not with you. What happened?"

He grabbed her hand. Startled, she pulled back, but he hung on.

"Mind if we go out on the porch, Sarah Anne?"

Sarah Anne? Something had to be wrong. Where was Zach? She immediately scanned the room, then remembered he'd gone to the barn with Sassy. "Fine. We can go on the porch." She did her best to read his expression, but to no avail. If anything, he looked suddenly shy and unsure of himself. Why?

Smoothing her skirt, she took the top step and settled her back against the wooden rail. TJ settled next to her, barely a breath away. "All right. I'm listening."

"I hope this isn't too personal, but I have a gift for you." He reached inside his coat pocket.

"A gift, for me?" Her hand fluttered over her heart. She hadn't received a gift since Nathaniel bought her the lamp. She reached for the small packet, and as their fingers touched, a warmth curled from his hand to hers. His eyes startled, and she figured hers must have done the same, because after a second he gave her a lazy smile.

When the flutters in her stomach wouldn't stop, she started to open the package to force her mind away from her feelings. Lifting the flap and turning the packet on its side, Sarah cried out when a ring and a watch fell into her hand. "TJ! How? How did you get these?"

"Sarah, you shouldn't have sold your ring. I wanted you to have them back."

Her heart thumped against her ribs, and her words

lodged in her throat. "Oh, TJ. I don't know how I'll ever repay you."

"One more thing." He stuffed his hand again into his pocket and pulled out a slip of paper. "I want you to have this."

"What is it?"

"Let's just say it's Zach's future."

Sarah licked her lips and opened the paper. "No! TJ, no! You can't do this. I won't let you." And then the realization hit. "You sold Saul, didn't you?"

"Well, I, uh… You see."

"Oh, TJ, how could you?" Since he'd come into their lives, he had helped with one problem after another. She'd been the biggest problem of all. He'd sold the horse he loved so much.

Without another word, TJ leaned forward and took the paper from Sarah's hands. He folded it and wedged it into a crack in the wood. His hands covered hers almost immediately. "Sarah, I want to clear up a few notions you might have about me."

"But, Preacher—"

"No buts. And don't call me Preacher. Just listen." He gazed into her eyes, daring her to look away, but she didn't. She couldn't. "I love you, Sarah. I would have helped you anyway, but I love you. I want to be here and help you, have you help me, every day of my life. I look forward to the chance to raise Zach with you. You must know how much I care about the boy. He's…well, he's almost like my own." He raised a hand. "Before you think I'm trying to take Nathaniel's place, it's not like that at all. I can't. I wouldn't even try. That's why I brought your ring back. You should have that to give to Zach one day. But I'd like the chance to put another ring on your finger. Won't be as fancy or as beautiful, but it's all I've got."

He pulled a plain gold band from his other pocket. "It was my mother's. All I have left of her now."

Sarah bit the edge of her lip. If only she had words to tell him how she felt, but words wouldn't come.

"I realize it's probably too soon, and, Sarah, I'm a greenhorn when it comes to women. I've never…well, I've never even kissed a woman till you. Not until last night. I'm afraid I'll be a big disappoint—"

Sarah wrapped her arms around his neck and pulled him to her until his heartbeat pounded in rhythm with hers. Did he feel it, too? His eyes raked her face, his breath sweet and warm against her cheeks.

His voice, husky and strong, whispered in her ear, "Oh, Sarah." Then he lowered his lips to hers. With a gentle brush, he skimmed across her mouth. Then, for this man who had always been nothing but gentle with her and Zach, he covered her mouth with his in an unexpected show of strength.

Soon she was lost in his protective power. Lost to his ever-present charm. At last he pulled away, but she clutched him closer. "No, kiss me again, TJ."

He nudged her away a few inches. "So I'm not too big a disappointment?"

She shook her head, focusing on his words. "Disappointment? TJ, I'd be happy if you disappointed me every day that way. Yes! Yes, I'd be proud to wear your mother's ring. And—" her face heated at her boldness "—to be your wife. But what about your promise? To God."

"I realized I had been bargaining with Him just like

I told you not to. I'd promised for the wrong reasons, Sarah. Now I think I'm where He wants me to be."

He crushed her to him again and they sat that way for what felt like hours, but it was only minutes before Zach ran toward them from the barn.

TJ sat straighter and leaned his elbows on his knees. What would the boy think about them becoming a family? Probably wouldn't want his mama to marry again. And he understood Zach not wanting a new pa.

Zach's face furrowed as he ran across the grass to the porch. "Whatcha doin' with Mama?"

He cleared his throat. "Well, I guess before I talk to your mama, I have to talk to you, Zach. Man to man, if it's all right."

With a suspicious glance, Zach looked first to TJ and then to his mama. "All right. I guess."

Lifting the boy to his shoulders, TJ galloped to the well and set the giggling Zach on the edge of the brick wall so Zach would appear taller. Then he lowered himself to one knee and smiled. "Zach, you're the man of the house now with your daddy gone, right?"

"Yes, sir. I am. Mama said so."

"And you do a right fine job of protecting her. I remember that first day when you were ready to throw a rock at me if I hurt your mama."

"Yes, sir, but you catcheded me."

TJ chuckled. "I did that. You're a good boy worth catching."

Zach puffed out his chest. "Thank you."

"Well, then, Zach, I'd like to have your permission to ask your mama if she'll marry me. Do you s'pose you'd let me ask her?"

The boy's face took on an expression of deep thought. Did he want a new daddy? Maybe he figured it would always be him and his mama from here on out. An uncomfortable length of time passed, and TJ cleared his throat at last. "Well? Would you give me your permission?"

"Would I! Ask her, Preacher. Ask her right now!"

"Let's ask her together. You and me."

Zach wrapped his arms around TJ's neck and hugged him close. "I always wanted a daddy. My whole life I wanted one."

TJ hugged him back. "And I've wanted a boy to raise ever since I met you and your mama." He lifted Zach onto his shoulders once again and trotted back to the porch.

With all the seriousness he could muster for this second proposal, he balanced Zach on his back while taking Sarah's hand. So Zach didn't notice, he quickly slipped the ring off and palmed it in his hand. "Sarah Anne Rycroft, will you do me the honor of becoming my wife? Let me help you raise Zach. Be my love, Sarah, forever."

Her eyes went from the laughing gaze TJ offered to what he expected to be a very serious expression on Zach's face.

"Well, Mama? Will you? Say yes."

Sarah enclosed them both in a hug, allowing her strength and goodness to flow from her heart straight to TJ's and, he suspected, Zach's, as well. "Yes, I'll marry you, TJ, and let you be part of our lives…forever."

"Mis-ter TJ, can I call you Pa after you marries her?"

Epilogue

Two months passed before TJ's friend, Robert Jennings, arrived in Gullywash for the wedding. TJ had wanted to be married right away, but Sarah longed to have a preacher marry them. As she said, it was for life, so God should be in the middle of their plans.

Her faith had grown so since the storm, and TJ realized what a gift God had given him in this woman. All of his fears about his lack of experience with women had faded that evening on Sarah's porch when he'd kissed her good-night after his proposal.

Her face willing and anxious, TJ had leaned down to peck her on the forehead, the only proper thing to do until they were engaged to be married, but Sarah had lifted those beautiful lips up to him and said, "I love you."

That was all he'd needed. His arms pulled her to him, the air whooshing from her, his lips hovering while he drank in her sweetness. "And I love you, Sarah Anne."

Then he'd kissed her with a passion he hadn't known existed in him. But it hadn't taken him long to discover the possibilities of what that meant.

Her eyes had melted into him. "Preacher O'Brien, I think you'd better be on your way home."

Instead he had held her tighter. "And why is that, Sarah Anne? I still don't know how to kiss?"

"Oh—" she had fanned her face playfully "—you surely know how."

He had been able to stop the laughter bubbling from deep inside as he'd stepped back and donned his hat with a flourish. "I had a mighty fine teacher, ma'am."

And she'd blushed, no doubt remembering the way she'd kissed him that first time.

Now here they were, standing before his best friend, Robert. Zach had walked her through the front room past their friends. Even Banker Studdard had found the gumption to show his face, though TJ wasn't sure how he had. But forgiveness had to be the first thing on his list if he was going to be a member of the community. All their church friends had jammed into Sarah's front room, their faces smiling, waiting as Robert Jennings pronounced TJ and Sarah husband and wife. Then TJ kissed her, and he kissed her good. He knew it was good from the shine in her eyes.

Zach, sitting on the sheriff's shoulders now that his job was done, clapped his hands and shouted, "I got me a new daddy!"

TJ grinned at the boy and then leaned in toward Sarah where no one else could hear. "And I got me a new wife. I love you, Sarah."

* * * * *

REQUEST YOUR FREE BOOKS!

2 FREE INSPIRATIONAL NOVELS
PLUS 2
FREE
MYSTERY GIFTS

Love Inspired

YES! Please send me 2 FREE Love Inspired® novels and my 2 FREE mystery gifts (gifts are worth about $10). After receiving them, if I don't wish to receive any more books, I can return the shipping statement marked "cancel." If I don't cancel, I will receive 6 brand-new novels every month and be billed just $4.74 per book in the U.S. or $5.24 per book in Canada. That's a savings of at least 21% off the cover price. It's quite a bargain! Shipping and handling is just 50¢ per book in the U.S. and 75¢ per book in Canada.* I understand that accepting the 2 free books and gifts places me under no obligation to buy anything. I can always return a shipment and cancel at any time. Even if I never buy another book, the two free books and gifts are mine to keep forever.

105/305 IDN F49N

Name	(PLEASE PRINT)	

Address		Apt. #

City	State/Prov.	Zip/Postal Code

Signature (if under 18, a parent or guardian must sign)

Mail to the **Harlequin® Reader Service:**
IN U.S.A.: P.O. Box 1867, Buffalo, NY 14240-1867
IN CANADA: P.O. Box 609, Fort Erie, Ontario L2A 5X3

Are you a subscriber to Love Inspired books
and want to receive the larger-print edition?
Call 1-800-873-8635 or visit www.ReaderService.com.

---

* Terms and prices subject to change without notice. Prices do not include applicable taxes. Sales tax applicable in N.Y. Canadian residents will be charged applicable taxes. Offer not valid in Quebec. This offer is limited to one order per household. Not valid for current subscribers to Love Inspired books. All orders subject to credit approval. Credit or debit balances in a customer's account(s) may be offset by any other outstanding balance owed by or to the customer. Please allow 4 to 6 weeks for delivery. Offer available while quantities last.

Your Privacy—The Harlequin® Reader Service is committed to protecting your privacy. Our Privacy Policy is available online at www.ReaderService.com or upon request from the Harlequin Reader Service.
We make a portion of our mailing list available to reputable third parties that offer products we believe may interest you. If you prefer that we not exchange your name with third parties, or if you wish to clarify or modify your communication preferences, please visit us at www.ReaderService.com/consumerchoice or write to us at Harlequin Reader Service Preference Service, P.O. Box 9062, Buffalo, NY 14269. Include your complete name and address.

LIDIR13R